UNDERCOVER AGENT

PHANTOM SECURITY: BOOK TWO

MARISSA DOBSON

Editors: Brynna Curry and Leigh Kirk
Proofers: Tammy Payne at Book Nook Nut, Teresa Riley, and Tammy Becraft
Published by Dobson Ink
Printed in the United States of America
ISBN-13: 978-1-946474-08-7

Dedication

To my husband. Thank you for all your support.

Chapter One

Bianca DeMeo lay in the dark bedroom, the only light coming from the glow of the bedside clock. Two twenty-three in the morning. Unsure of what woke her, she cuddled against her boyfriend and listened. As if on cue, Anthony draped his arm over her midsection, pulling her closer to his body as he slept. His presence should have put her at ease, but she couldn't shake the tightness in her stomach. Something wasn't right. Her heart raced as she peered around the room, her ears working overtime searching for any sound. With each moment that passed her anxiety rose. Just as she was about to wake him, a loud bang echoed downstairs. It reminded her of when she bumped the door too hard sending it back against the wall. She bolted upright, terrified of who it could be.

She felt Anthony shift beside her.

"Under there. Now." Now alert and rising from the bed, Anthony grabbed a gun from the nightstand drawer.

After she started spending the night with him, he had explained what she should do if anything ever happened, but she never expected to act on it. She always assumed he was being overly cautious. Now as she slipped down onto the floor and crawled into the hidey-hole under the solid wood bedframe, she realized how dangerous things might actually have become. *Marco.*

"I love you," he whispered as she slid the latch into place, locking herself inside. There was no chance anyone would find her, unless she undid the latch or they tore the bed apart.

She wanted to tell him she loved him, too, but fear kept her mute. With only enough room for her to lay flat on her back, she turned her head toward where he'd be standing. Through a small crack in the frame, she saw his ankles. Even though she couldn't touch him, she reached out to him, tears welling in her eyes. Her heart shattered as if this was the end. She wanted to climb out and go to him. They had something special, and she didn't care if Marco agreed with it or not. It was her life; she deserved to be happy.

"FBI! Drop the gun!" a deep voice yelled.

FBI? What are they doing here? She tried to get a better view, but no matter how she adjusted she couldn't see who was in the doorway. The thump of Anthony's weapon against the wood floor pulled her attention back to him. Was this really the FBI or more of Marco's bullshit? Fear spiked within her, her heart pounding as she waited for gunshots to ring out and for Anthony to fall to the floor.

"Take a step back, turn around, and get on your knees."

"What's this about?" Anthony's calm tone warred against the anger laced throughout it.

"Get on the ground, now."

"What—" before Anthony could finish the question, a hand pushed him forward until he was face down on the floor. Anger and confusion simmered in his gaze but there was something more. Fear. Was he afraid for himself or for her? Knowing him, it was for her but she was terrified for him.

"Chris Weaver, you're under arrest. You have the right to remain silent..." The rest of the words faded into the background. As their gazes locked onto each other, she saw the man she knew as Anthony but was his name actually Chris Weaver? Why had he lied to her? Was it possible the FBI had the wrong man?

Unsure how much of her he could see, she reached out to him until her fingers brushed along the smooth wood. Tears slid down her cheek and her chest tightened, making it hard to breathe. She wanted to brush her fingers along his skin, to have his arms wrapped around her, but there was a chance she'd never experience that again.

"Murdering asshole. Did you really think we wouldn't catch you? I hope you enjoyed your time out. Escaping from prison might not add anything to your life-without-parole sentence, asshole, but now you're going to Supermax. You fucked up."

"He's a cold-blooded murderer. He deserves what's coming to him." Another agent came into the room.

"You have the wrong man; I'm not Chris Weaver. Check the dresser."

She wanted to scream out his name as they hauled him to his feet. Frozen in place, her heart shattered as they dragged him away. In the distance, she heard him arguing with the agents. He begged anyone to believe him, but they weren't responding. Were they even listening to him?

Escaped from prison? Chris Weaver? Murder? Supermax? None of it made sense. They'd started dating six months ago. During that time, he'd been wrapped up with her brother, Marco, and that was dangerous enough, but she couldn't picture him as a murderer.

I can't believe the man I love is a murderer. I'll prove he's not.

Chapter Two

Welcome to Hell. Undercover work had been tortuous at times, but it was nothing compared to the trouble Paxton Payne found himself in now. He couldn't name a single place worse than where he was—prison. Every day brought a new set of challenges, another asshole trying to end his life and claim the bounty on his head. Someone put a call out to end his life, and if forced to guess, Marco Nitti topped the list. Paxton must have been closer to the truth than he had realized, and now rather than doing his job at Phantom Security, he found himself in lock up. *Why haven't they gotten me out yet? What's taken Rocco so long?*

"You know the routine, Weaver." The older of the two guards nudged Paxton through the door into solitary confinement. Over the last several weeks, he'd gone through this more times than he wanted to remember.

He didn't bother trying to convince the guard Chris Weaver wasn't his name. What proof could he offer? Instead, he went through the routine, and as the metal door closed, he tried to keep his mind blank. Every time he found himself locked in another cage, he wondered why he fought so hard to stay alive. Convincing people of the truth proved harder than he imagined, and he'd barely made it twenty-four hours before he found himself back in the hole again.

Standing with his back to the door, his fingers brushed against the cool metal tray as he waited for the guards to unlock his cuffs. The slot in the door served as his only connection to the people outside solitary confinement, it allowed the guards to cuff him and hand him his meals. A dog locked in a cage and some wondered why the prisoners came out worse than they went in.

"Four days…that's the longest you've lasted." The guard slid the key into the handcuffs and unhooked them from Paxton's wrists. "I knew it wouldn't last. When are you going to learn fighting will get you nowhere but back here?"

What was he supposed to say to that? He didn't enjoy being in the hole, but it was either that or find himself flat on his back in a casket. His family and friends wouldn't even know he died. His undercover identity labeled him as a criminal without a family. If he died in prison, he'd end up in a pauper's grave. That wasn't how he wanted to end his life. He wanted his life back so he kept his mouth shut and pulled his arms back from the tray, allowing the guard to shut it.

The guards stepped away from the door and the countdown for the first forty-eight hours began. In that time, he'd have no contact with another human being, except when they passed his meals through the slot, but no words would be exchanged. Even after the initial timeframe, he was looking at a week, if not longer, in the hole with only an hour of rec time each day. He didn't need to look around the cell to know the four-by-eight room would close in around him before the door opened again.

This punishment was meant to break a person, to tear him down so he'd fall in line. For Paxton, knowing he wouldn't have to watch his back or sleep with one eye open provided a small amount of relief. The hole was a double-edged sword, bringing its own set of challenges and the biggest was not losing his mind before release day. There was nothing good about being locked in the cell completely alone, yet it was his only way to survive. Behind these walls there didn't seem to be a single person he could trust. His attempts to reach his boss, Rocco, had been unsuccessful.

He sank onto the bed—a concrete slab with a thin mattress on top—and tried to determine his next move. He had tried to convince anyone who would listen that he wasn't the man they wanted without success. How could he when his image and fingerprints matched the name of Chris Weaver?

He hadn't realized how far Marco's reach went until the FBI had broken down his door in the middle of the night, hauling him off to prison as an escaped convict sentenced to serve life without the chance of parole. Didn't any of these guards or inmates realize he wasn't this Weaver who had escaped? Maybe there had never been a Chris Weaver.

Anger coursed through his veins, threatening to overwhelm him. Paxton clenched his hands into tight fists. *Accepting this fate isn't an option, I have to find a way out of here and back to Bianca.* He remembered his father's last words to him, spoken as he'd boarded the bus to boot camp. *Don't give up…never give up.* Now more than ever, he needed to hold onto those words. *I'll find a way back to you Bianca, I swear.*

Chapter Three

Bianca DeMeo stepped into the lobby of Phantom Security, her heart a hurricane of emotions; the folder of evidence clutched tight in her hand. Her stomach churned as she forced herself to walk forward. *I actually made it. I'm finally here.* Only one option presented itself, meeting with Rocco Arquette and gaining a promise to help. An innocent man's life hung in the balance.

"Ma'am, are you okay?" A young blonde rose from behind the reception desk and pulled off her hands-free headset as she came around the solid wood desk.

"I…" Bianca's throat felt dry as she fought for control over her emotions. "I need to speak with Mr. Arquette."

In an instant, the concern disappeared and the receptionist's back straightened. "I'm afraid that's impossible. However, I can set you up with an appointment." She stepped back around her desk, sat down, and tapped keys as she glanced down at the screen. "His first available appointment is two weeks from Friday at one o'clock. Shall I put you down?"

"It's Monday. That's almost three weeks from now." Bianca shook her head, refusing to settle for that. "My business with Mr. Arquette can't wait that long."

"I'm sorry, but without an appointment, I'm afraid there's nothing I can do. I've been given strict orders he's not to be disturbed. Perhaps someone else could speak with you."

"You don't understand. I have to speak with him!" Bianca's voice rose louder, causing a scene, but she couldn't stop. She had exhausted all other avenues. This was her last hope. "Trust me; he'll want the information I have."

"I can get another agent—"

"It's an emergency!" She slammed her hand down on the glossy black desk.

"Chelsea, is there a problem here?" A woman with long, reddish-brown hair strolled toward them from a hallway off to the side.

"No, Elise, I was explaining to her that Mr. Arquette is occupied and is unable to meet with her at this time. I offered to get another agent." The receptionist's gaze never left Bianca.

"Elise? You're Elise Arquette? Please…" Instantly recognizing Elise from the pictures online of her and the two Arquette brothers, she stepped away from the desk and focused on the new woman. Phantom Security was well known for their elite security. Rumor had it they handled jobs the government couldn't. The legal limits might be blurry but when it came to right and wrong they were firmly on the right side. They'd do what needed to be done, no matter the cost. They had the right supports in place to allow them to continue to push the bounds. Elise was married to Flash, the younger brother. She could help Bianca. Determination flowed through her. "Please, I need to speak with your husband or Rocco. I have information they'll want."

"They're both busy at the moment. Maybe we can—"

"Paxton…I know where Paxton Payne is." She grabbed Elise's arm, begging her to recognize the desperation in her eyes. "Please, he needs your help. I need your help."

"Security." The receptionist's voice barely registered as Bianca watched Elise's expression change.

"What's your name?" Elise raised her eyebrow as if trying to determine whether or not she was telling the truth.

"Bianca DeMeo." Elise's gaze shot back to her as if she recognized her name. "You know my name, don't you?"

"Chelsea, cancel the call to security. I'm going to take Ms. DeMeo back to the conference room." Elise turned. "Come with me and we'll find somewhere more private where we can talk."

Clenching the folder, she followed Elise down the hall. Scared they'd turn her away without even hearing her out, she went over the highlights of what she had to tell them. If security dragged her out before she could give them everything she learned, she needed to make sure they at least knew some of the important details. She was Paxton's one chance and it was up to her not to blow it.

"Jac, just the person I need." Elise called to a tall man in jeans and a button-down shirt as he stepped into the hall.

"If I had a dime for every time I heard that." He chuckled. "Should I fetch you a coffee, Mrs. Arquette? Or perhaps you're taking the rest of the day off? The joys of being married to the boss." With a grin on his face, he leaned against the doorframe, clearly teasing.

"You're jealous I outrank you now," she jabbed back. "Seriously, get Flash and Rocco for me. It's important. Have them meet me in conference room two." Without waiting for him to answer, she pulled open a door and allowed Bianca to enter first. "Take a seat."

"How do you know who I am?" Bianca pulled out the first chair on the side of the rectangle table, dropped the bag she had slung over her shoulder to the floor and sat. With a quick glance, she took in the room. She hadn't been in many conference rooms before, but it was what she would have expected. Very business-like with leather, high-back chairs surrounding a long black and steel table. Cream walls stood out against the hardwood floor, the only accent of color was a small table with a red tablecloth along the wall. Holding a thermos for coffee, it appeared to be a place for refreshments if the occasion called for it.

"How do you know Paxton?" Elise ignored Bianca's question and took a seat at the head of the table.

"It's complicated. Let's say he means a great deal to me, and he needs your help."

"You're going to need to tell me more if you want our help," Elise informed her as the door to the conference room opened.

Even knowing no one from Marco's team would venture into Phantom Security, she couldn't stop herself from going still at the new arrivals. Every time a door opened, she expected to find one of Marco's men on the other side, waiting to kill her. Instead, Flash and Rocco entered.

"I thought you were going to get coff—" Flash's gaze slid to Bianca, stopping him mid-sentence. "Impossible."

"Are you Bianca DeMeo?" Rocco asked after he shut the door behind them. "What are you doing here?"

"She claims to have information on Paxton," Elise supplied.

"He needs your help." Bianca clutched the folder in her lap and let out a deep sigh. "I came here prepared with what I needed to say. Now that we're face-to-face, I don't know where to begin. Everything I thought was important to tell you now seems like it will only leave you more confused."

"Start at the beginning." Rocco came around the table to join them. "We'll listen to whatever you need to tell us."

"He's in prison," Bianca blurted out.

"Impossible." Flash placed his hand on the back of his wife's chair. "The system would have flagged his name on any court documents and alerted us."

"I doubt you have it set to alert you for the name Chris Weaver." Sliding her chair up to the table, she placed the folder in front of her. "Paxton Payne, Anthony Davis, Chris Weaver…it's all so complicated, but they're all the same person. They're all Paxton, maybe there are more. To me, he was Anthony."

"You knew him through your brother Marco?" Flash questioned.

"No…not at first. You have no reason to believe me, but I don't want anything to do with my brother's lifestyle. I didn't even know my father was part of the mafia until he died. That's when Marco took over for him. I guess our father had been grooming him for the position for some time. Through all of it, they kept me sheltered from it. I suspected my father wasn't on the right side of the law, but I never imagined he was doing what he was." She shook her head and focused her attention back on Elise. "There was this coffee shop a few blocks away from my condo. The coffee was amazing and for a short time every day, I could visit and pretend to be normal. That's how I first met Anthony. We'd say hi, but that was all for weeks. One day I was late, and by the time I arrived, he was already sitting there with his muffin and coffee. He seemed different, uneasy. I invited myself to sit down at his table. I wanted to cheer him up. That's how it started, and before I knew it, he was something more."

"You didn't know he worked for Marco?" Elise asked.

"Not until two weeks later when Marco requested me to attend a dinner in honor of an out-of-town guest. I was ordered to be ready at seven o'clock, and my bodyguard for the night would pick me up at my condo. Anthony showed up at my door and he was as surprised as I was. Just like I didn't know he was working for my brother, he didn't know I was Marco's sister. I'm not sure who was more upset by the revelation. I wanted something better for him. Working for Marco would not end well. Still, we didn't break things off. We snuck around behind my brother's back."

"Did he find out?" Elise pushed when Bianca fell silent.

"I never suspected anything until Anthony was arrested. Hours after the arrest, Marco called me, angry I had betrayed him. He believed I was giving Anthony information about the family business. Except I knew nothing about any of it. As Marco ranted he complained about Mayor Folger, how he was trying to set him up. I didn't know what he was talking about until now. Now I know the whole thing's a setup." She pushed the folder to Elise. "Paxton was hired to find Mayor Folger's missing niece, except she isn't missing. She's tucked away in a house an hour outside of Chicago. The Mayor used Anthony to get information to further his plans to bring down the organization. While I can support his reasons, he's doing it at the cost of Anthony, and I can't stand by and allow it to happen. I need your help. You have the power to stop this."

"You said Paxton is in prison under the name of Chris Weaver. How does this tie in?" Rocco glanced down at his phone for a moment before looking back up at her. "Paxton went undercover as Anthony Davis, but even with his past jobs, the alias Chris Weaver has never been used."

"After everything we've read about Marco Nitti, I figure he's smart enough to know we'd have flagged Paxton and Anthony in the system to make sure we received any alerts if either name came up." Elise opened the folder Bianca handed her. "There's something we're missing."

"Marco didn't want to give you time to get him out. He has people in high places. He used those connections to create a false record. The prisoner, Chris Weaver, was doing life in prison for murder before he was killed in a prison fight. I saw proof Marco had the identification changed to make it appear that Anthony is Chris. This was his way of getting Anthony out of the way and having him taken care of behind bars."

Elise leaned forward and pressed a couple of buttons on the phone before bringing it to her ear. "Jac, I need you to get everything you can on a prisoner named Chris Weaver. He's doing life in prison without the possibility of parole. When you get it, bring it down to the conference room."

"Since Chris Weaver has already been convicted, it's going to be harder to get Paxton out." Rocco scooted his chair closer to Elise to peruse the file.

"Harder but not impossible. Our connections go deeper than Marco's, and we're sure as fuck not going to let one of our guys spend the rest of his life in prison." Flash gripped the back of the chair until his knuckles whitened. "Fuck, Rocco, I told you something wasn't right around the job."

"Hey now." Elise turned to her husband. "We're going to get him out."

"El, you have no idea…"

She rose to stand in front of him. "Flash—"

"Don't." His voice was low as he pulled her into his embrace.

"If you need…" Rocco tipped his head toward the door, but when Flash shook his head, he turned back to Bianca. "How did you find out he was undercover and end up coming to us?"

She slipped her hand into her bag and pulled out a folded envelope. "When he showed me the hidey-hole under the bedframe, I thought he was being paranoid. Maybe he was concerned Marco would come there and I'd need somewhere to hide. I don't know, but I never expected to have to use it. When the noise woke us, he told me to get in there. I moved the board out of the way, and once I was inside, I locked it into place as he had told me to do. By the time I was sure everyone was gone and it was safe to come out, the sun was rising, casting a glow bright enough I spotted this."

She withdrew the single piece of paper before carefully unfolding it and laying it out on the table. *If you're finding this, we're already up shit creek, and for that, I'm sorry. From the first day I saw you sitting there in the café, I knew you were it for me. Your smile brightens up even the darkest part of me, and you've made me believe there's something more to life. Every day that passes makes telling you the truth harder, but I never wanted you to find out like this. I hope you'll give me the chance to explain. If I'm already dead, find Rocco Arquette. Maybe he can explain things to you and you'll find it in your heart to forgive me. No matter where I am or what happens, you'll always be my girl. My one slice of happiness. I love you, Bianca.*

Knowing the words written on the page by heart, she handed the note to Rocco. Reading it aloud would break the fragile shell she had wrapped around her emotions, and she couldn't afford that. Even as Rocco's gaze scanned the page, the words echoed through her thoughts as though Anthony stood there speaking them. If she closed her eyes, she knew he'd fill her vision.

"At first, I thought he meant he was Chris Weaver, even then I couldn't believe he was a cold-blooded killer. The Anthony I knew was different…he couldn't have…" She shook her head, unable to explain further. "It was as if someone ripped out my heart. I was hurt, scared, and part of me was broken, yet I refused to give up without some proof. I didn't want to believe it. When the FBI arrived, I figured Marco had something to do with it. I couldn't explain how Marco could pull it off. To get Anthony arrested on murder charges, sure I could see that, but to have him already tried and convicted, seemed beyond him. I planned to confront Marco, but as I was getting dressed, I remembered the bag in the back of his closet."

"His go-bag," Elise supplied.

"Yeah, that's what he called it. A few days before, he added some of my things into it. He said it was a precaution in case we had to run. It made me realize if I went to Marco, I wouldn't like the outcome. I didn't believe my brother would kill me, but now, I think he might. I knew he had ways to get to Anthony. So, I ran without a plan on what to do. Every town I went I spotted someone who worked for Marco. Anthony's letter said to find Rocco Arquette but I didn't think about it then. I was focused on running and I didn't know who you were or even about Phantom Security."

"Paxton was paranoid?" Flash shifted slightly, bringing Elise more at his side, so he could take in Bianca.

"He told me it was nothing, but he was more on edge. Marco became more unreasonable. It got to the point Marco wanted me to come stay at the house, but I refused. I asked Anthony if he thought Marco knew about our relationship but he said it was something else. He wouldn't explain, but I trusted him. If we were in immediate danger, he'd have told me."

"How long ago was this?" Rocco's questioning gaze stayed on her.

"Four weeks ago, we suspected he knew, but a week had passed without incident." Uncomfortable she shifted in her chair. "I thought it was over. Then the FBI busted down Anthony's door."

"Timeline fits." Elise turned to Rocco. "It's been three weeks since Paxton missed check-in."

"Three weeks and one day since he was arrested." With everyone's attention back on her, she was forced to swallow past the lump forming in her throat. "I put the pieces together after I found this."

Lifting the bag off the floor, she brought it into her lap and unzipped the side pocket. As her fingers closed around the smooth plastic card, she turned it so she could see Anthony's smiling face again. "Tucked away at the bottom of his go-bag was his Phantom Security badge. It was hidden in a small rip in the lining. I'd been running from Marco's men for weeks when I couldn't go on any longer. I found a cash only motel for the night. I was tired of sleeping in abandoned buildings and wanted a hot shower and a real bed. After the shower, I was rummaging through the bag, looking for clean clothes when my fingernail caught on the material. I was checking to make sure I didn't rip the bag when I found the card. It was early Friday morning, and by nightfall, I realized I needed to come here."

She sat the bag back on the floor and turned her attention to Rocco. "He trusted you to explain things to me if he ended up dead, so I think he'd believe you'd help me now. Mayor Folger sent him to work with my brother, knowing his niece was safe, now he's in prison. He doesn't deserve that. Maybe Anthony was using me to get information about Marco or to get back at him. I'm not sure, but there are two things I do know. One, Marco is responsible for Anthony being in prison and the other is I'm in love with Anthony."

"Do you have proof Marco is behind this?" Flash asked.

"Everything I have is in the folder." She tipped her head toward the folder she slid to Elise. "You'll see. Marco used his connections to change the information for a convicted murderer who was killed in a prison fight. Anthony's fingerprints and image were used to replace the original man's, but there are original documents as well."

Rocco reached across the table to the folder and began skimming through the information. "How did you get this information?"

"Anthony's laptop." She ran her finger over the Phantom Security badge she held in her hand. "I don't know how he did it, but it's like a clone of Marco's computer. I don't know why I grabbed the laptop as I left, but when I found the badge I turned it on to research you. That's when I found all of this."

"Where's the laptop?" Elise stepped away from Flash and came back to the table. "I need it."

"Will you get him out of prison?" Bianca held tight to the bag strap in her hand. There was no way she was giving up the only evidence she had without their promise to help. "I'll go to the police with the information…"

"And you'll both be dead before the day's over," Flash warned.

Even though she knew he was speaking the truth, his words sent a chill through her. She might end up dead because of this; Marco's men had already tried. As long as she got him out of prison that was what mattered. *Don't give up, Anthony. I'm working on it.*

Chapter Four

Sitting around the conference room waiting for someone to return was driving Bianca stir crazy. She might be safer here than out on the streets waiting for one of Marco's men to find her, but it was making her uneasy. Anything could be happening while she was stuck waiting. *I feel so helpless!* They said they believed her and would help but what if it was a lie?

Standing next to the wall of windows, the skyline of New York City blurred as her panic began to take over. She was close to losing everything, and the only thing she cared about was Anthony. She wanted him back; actually, she wanted to go back in time. Even if he got out of prison, it didn't mean she'd have him back.

"He probably doesn't even care about me. Maybe I was part of his cover. Or he thought he could get closer to the information he wanted with me by his side?" She pressed her hand to the cool glass and fought to tame her emotions.

"I've known Paxton for years. He's not that type of man." She spun around to see Rocco standing in the doorway. "I didn't mean to startle you."

"Done with your background search on me?" She tried not to let her annoyance show. When she decided to come, she knew they'd look into her. It would have been stupid not to and would have made her think less of Phantom Security. Her family had a long history in the Chicago mafia; she could have been sent in retaliation for them sending Paxton undercover.

"We'd already started researching you before you arrived." Rocco strolled in and shut the door behind him. "Paxton and I go way back. I knew there was something he was not being forthcoming about. I didn't expect you to be what he was hiding, but now, it makes sense."

"Why?"

"He knows the rules. You don't get emotionally involved when undercover. Eventually, the job will be over, and it's going to end. Relationships are hard enough in our line of work but add in more complications, and you are dooming yourself. Relationships are built on trust. How can one built on a lie survive?"

"Not much for romance, are you?"

"Don't act like you're not doubting everything between the two of you. I overheard a bit of your doubt, and I'm positive that's only a sliver of what you're thinking." He rested his hands on the back of one of the chairs.

"What do you want from me? Do you want me to say I'm not sure what was real and what was an act? Fine, it's true. I don't know, but unless we find a way to get him out of prison, I'll never know." She stepped away from the window and came toward Rocco, keeping the table between them. "I'd like a few answers from him before Marco's men get their hands on me. Now, are you going to help or not?"

"We're working on it." His brows knitted together as he watched her.

"Good, then I'll check in with you when I can." She bent over to grab her bag when she caught movement out of the corner of her vision and glanced up to find Rocco coming around the table. Before she could stop herself, she took a step back, dragging the bag across the hardwood floor. "I don't want any trouble."

"Whoa, what gives you that impression?" He held his hands up, as if surrendering. "I was coming to take your bag. It's the gentleman in me. You've been through a lot in the last few weeks. Let me help you."

"In exchange for what? I've already offered you everything I could find to get you to help Anthony…or Paxton…or whatever you want to call him. Elise has the laptop. I don't have anything else to offer you. I'm sure you can find everything you need on the computer to ruin Marco, you don't need me." She hefted the bag up onto her shoulder. "I'll be fine."

"This isn't about needing your help or even bringing down your brother." He dragged his hand through his hair, moving the silky black strands away from his face. "Whether you want to face it or not, you're in danger. It's clear you mean a lot to Paxton. He'd want you protected."

"I can handle it."

"Really? Then let me show you something." He pulled out his phone from the pocket of his slacks and held it out to her. "Recognize anyone?"

She stared down at the screen, her eyes locking in on the man in the center of the screen. Her brain refused to comprehend what she was seeing. Maybe it was a prank, a trick with two different photos merging them together. They couldn't have found her so soon; once she lost them, she always had a little time before they found her again. She should have at least another day if not two.

"Follow me to my office, and I'll bring up the live screen. I'm sure he's still there. I checked the footage; he's been outside the building for over an hour now. He knows you're here, and he's waiting." The phone screen dimmed, and he touched the corner, brightening it back up. "You still want to leave?"

"That's…" She couldn't get the words to come out.

"Gino."

Gino had worked his way up to his position as capo, leaving a long bloody trail behind him. There was something that had always terrified her about him, although she had once thought Marco would have killed Gino for hurting her. The way he looked at her sent chills racing over her skin. If her brother had sent him, she didn't stand a chance. Marco didn't want to tame her and put her back in place; he wanted her dead. Gino wouldn't kill her quickly, which terrified her more. In his hands, she would suffer horrors she couldn't bear to think about.

"Now will you let me help you?" Rocco locked the phone screen and slipped it back into his pocket. "You're not going to live long enough to be reunited with Paxton otherwise."

"Why would you help me?" With the fight gone from her, she let go of the bag and pulled out a chair. "You've got what you need to stop Marco—"

"Marco was never on our radar. We don't give a fuck about him." He pulled out the chair beside her and sat.

"What do you mean? Why else was Anthony, I mean Paxton, there other than to help further Mayor Folger's agenda?"

"The mayor is a friend of Paxton's father. The job was a favor for him. We believed there was an innocent girl's life at stake, which is why I agreed to it. I didn't start Phantom Security to go up against the mafia. That's Chicago's issue, not ours." He reached out and took her hand. "I have no interest in your brother, but you need to know the information you gave us will be turned over to the authorities. We're going to have to use it in order to get Paxton out of prison."

Leaning back in the chair, she waited a moment to allow his words to sink in, but there was no effect on her. "I don't care. I've never supported the life he lives, and I want no part of it. It is only a matter of time before everything he's done catches up to him. More than that, he's screwed with…" She couldn't bring herself to say, *with the man I love*. It was true. She couldn't stop the fear from rising within her that he didn't feel the same, or worse, he wasn't the same man.

"Come on then." He reached down to her bag but stopped before grabbing hold of it. "May I?"

She nodded. "Where are we going?"

"The penthouse, two floors up. You're going to stay with me."

"Stay with you?" she asked as he rose with her bag in his hand.

"Yes, until it's safe. Besides the general security guards for the building, I have round-the-clock guards that monitor my top floors, including my penthouse. You'll be safe up there. After next week, if you'd be more comfortable in one of the condos on the floor below, we can arrange it, but they're occupied now. I want you safe, and upstairs is where I can ensure your safety. You should stay until we get Paxton back; you'll be safe here."

"You make it sound like it's going to take some time to free him."

He waited for her to stand before answering. "We all want him home, now, but that's not how this will work. I've got to go about this the right way, or it's going to delay the process. Elise and Flash are verifying the information, and I believe we know what prison he's being held at. Once they have all the loose ends tied up, I'll contact those who can help."

"Is there anything I can do?"

"Give me your phone." He paused by the door and held out his hand. "I'll get you another one, but this one I'm sure Marco can track. That's probably how they found you, unless they've been on your tail."

She pulled the phone from her pocket and handed it to him. "I figured that, so I shut it off, but I kept it in case…I thought Anthony might call."

"Depending on what technology Marco uses, he still might be able to track you even if it's off. We're going to destroy it, but as long as you're here, you'll know if Paxton contacts us. Prison calls have a time limit, so I can't promise you'll be able to speak with him, but I'll do my best." He shoved her phone into his pocket and opened the door.

"Shouldn't he have called? Don't you have some kind of protocol if something happens? Could he be…oh shit!"

Rocco shut the door and turned back to her. "Don't, Bianca, don't think

27

like that."

"But if he hasn't called—"

"No." He placed his hand on her shoulder, squeezing it slightly. "There's going to be a logical reason why he hasn't called. We'll get to the bottom of this, and I'll bring him home."

She hadn't considered what it might mean if Anthony hadn't contacted Rocco or anyone at Phantom Security. It had been weeks since he was taken, he should have contacted someone by now. Either by phone, or mail. Something. The lack of communication was more alarming than watching him being handcuffed and hauled away by those agents. What if he was dead? Had she lost him already and didn't know it?

The hole should have lifted some of the weight from Paxton's shoulders, allowing him a moment to think of a way out of this situation. Yet his thoughts were filled with Bianca. She was the one woman he never should have had, but the only one he ever wanted. The moment he laid eyes on her, he was a goner.

Undercover work was difficult. He had to leave behind his life, family, and friends—essentially, he was alone—yet he wasn't supposed to build relationships with those who surrounded him. Eventually, his undercover mission would have ended, and any connections he established would be destroyed. He wanted it to be different with Bianca, but the moment he found out who she was, he knew any chance was gone. If the mission were successful, he'd be the man responsible for placing her brother behind bars. She'd never be able to forgive him. Even then, that was only the beginning of the betrayal. He had no doubt she would believe their relationship had been built on lies. And it had, but not completely. He lied about his name, but the person he was when he was with her, that had been real. Without meaning to, he had fallen in love with Bianca.

"*Anthony…*" Her voice was barely above a whisper as she called to him. Needing the escape, he closed his eyes and allowed the memory to fill him.

"What are you doing here?"

Standing in the doorway to her condo, she took his breath away. The simple black dress hugged her curves, while her long, dark brown hair was curled and flowed freely around her shoulders, making him want to tangle his fingers in it as he brought her mouth to his. With just enough makeup to highlight her natural beauty and a pair of gold hoop earrings, she was sure to take any man's breath away. She was gorgeous, which brought out his protective side. The idea of men ogling her throughout this dinner with Marco nearly sent him into a rage. He wanted to force her back inside, to call Marco with an excuse she was sick, anything to keep her away from what he knew would happen.

"Is everything okay, Anthony?" She reached out and placed her hand on his forearm. "I don't have a lot of time, I'm waiting for my ride."

"It would seem I'm your ride." He took a step closer so their bodies were almost touching. "Marco sent me."

"I…um…what?"

"Inside." He escorted her inside, quickly shutting the door behind them before pressing her back against the wall. "Why didn't you tell me you were his sister?"

"I…" Her mouth was still open as she stared up at him. "Wait. Why didn't you tell me you worked for him?"

"You know I couldn't." His hand slid along her hip, inching further up her body.

"Oh, Anthony…" She leaned into him, pressing her head against his chest. "I don't want this for you."

"Come on, we should go. Marco's expecting you." He pressed his lips to the top of her head before stepping back. They had been dating each other for a few weeks. This development wasn't something he expected. Until that morning, he never knew Marco had a sister. Mayor Folger never mentioned it, and none of the investigations Phantom Security did turned up a sibling. How had they missed this?

"I never meant to deceive you. I just didn't know how to tell you." She tucked a strand of hair behind her ear and stepped away from the wall. "This part of my family history was hidden from me until my father died."

"Later. We need to go; Marco isn't a man who likes to be kept waiting."

"Anthony, you need to know—"

He touched her arm, silencing her. "I know everything I need to, and this changes nothing between us. If you want to tell me more, then you can later."

The memory shifted, quickly sending him their last moments together.

The echo of the front door splintering off the hinges moments before it landed with a thud on the floor sent him bolting upright. His paranoia about Marco being suspicious of him sprang to mind. The only thing that seemed to explain what was happening was Marco's men were there for him, and he couldn't allow them to find Bianca in bed with him.

Out of the corner of his gaze, she stood by the bed with only his t-shirt on. Her long hair tangled from sleep, and her eyes wide with fear as she stared at him.

"Get under there. Now." Without waiting to see if she listened, he pulled his gun from the nightstand drawer. They had been through the precautionary measures he had put in place to protect her enough so he wasn't concerned she'd ignore him. She was terrified of Marco and his men, so she'd do as ordered.

As the latch slid into place with a soft click, he knew she'd be safe there. No one would realize there was a hiding spot under the solid wood bedframe. Not knowing what would happen, he wanted her to know how he felt. Keeping his voice low, he whispered, "I love you."

He would have given anything for her to say it back, but as men stormed his room, he was grateful she remained quiet. He brought his gun up as the first man, completely in black, entered.

"FBI! Drop the gun!" a deep voice hollered.

"What the fuck? Let me see some ID." He had a split second before two others joined the first man. He was out gunned, and if he didn't put his weapon down, he'd be dead before he could determine if it was really the FBI or some fucked up game Marco was playing. Not

wanting to end up bleeding out while Bianca watched, he put the gun down and put his hands in the air. If it was the FBI, this would be over quick. He had nothing to worry about.

"Take a step back, turn around, and get on your knees."

"What's this about?" He did as they asked.

"Get on the ground, now."

"What—" Before he could finish the question, a hand shoved his back hard, forcing him down onto the ground.

"Chris Weaver, you're under arrest. You have the right to remain silent..."

Face down on the hard floor as they handcuffed him, he stared at the bed frame. He wasn't sure if it was his mind playing tricks on him or if he was going crazy, but he swore he caught a glimpse of her hand pressed against the wood, as if she was reaching out to him.

As the handcuffs tightened against his wrists, the reality of the situation struck him. Chris Weaver? What the fuck? "You've got the wrong person."

"Murdering asshole, did you really think we wouldn't catch you? I hope you enjoyed your time out. Escaping from prison might not add anything to your life without parole sentence, asshole, but now you're going to Supermax. You fucked up."

Life in prison. Murder. Fuck no. He tried to speak, but another agent cut him off.

"He's a cold-blooded murderer. He deserves what's coming to him." Another agent strolled into the room.

"Listen to me. You have the wrong man. I'm not Chris Weaver. Check the dresser."

They hauled him to his feet before quickly dragging him off. No one listened to him, and his wallet was left behind on the dresser, proving who he was. As they threw him into the back of the SUV, he caught a glimpse of Gino across the street, hanging back in the shadows. Stay where you are, Bianca.

The sight of Gino left little doubt in his mind that somehow this all tied back to Marco. He needed to get to the station and call Rocco. He might be able to prove he wasn't who they thought he was when they fingerprinted him, but until then, someone needed to watch over Bianca. He didn't give a fuck if his secret would be exposed; he wanted her protected. She meant more to him than anything else. I'll be back for you, Bianca, and I'll prove to you I love you more than anything else. I'll get you to forgive me for everything.

An earsplitting scream from one of the neighboring cells popped the memory like a bubble, forcing him to return to the reality of his solitary. Grabbing the thin material the prison officials called a blanket, he wrapped it around himself as he tried to fight off the constant chill in the air. Since the basement of the prison housed the hole, the temperature remained ten degrees colder than his normal cell. The cinder blocks only added to the cold, and the stench of mildew lingered in the stale air.

It hadn't even been twenty-four hours, and he was already seeing Bianca before him and hearing her name. The hole was getting to him, driving him crazy. Being locked up in a cage for twenty-three hours a day like a dangerous animal was almost more than his mind could take. He understood how some people could lose their sanity there. It was maddening to be here, and he could only hope he wasn't one of them. He leaned back on the hard bunk and closed his eyes. Without even trying, Bianca's image filled his vision.

He wasn't sure how he'd ever make it back to her, but thinking about her helped him get through his days. She was the one good thing in his life. He never expected to find someone like her, especially not while undercover, surrounded by criminals, as he worked to bring home Mayor Folger's niece. She was innocent, and to have her stuck in that life made him want to take her and leave. The only thing that had kept him there was knowing more innocent women were forced into the cellars of Hell. Women who had no idea the horrors awaiting them until they were sold off to the highest bidder. Sex trafficking started his mission, yet even after six months of working undercover, he could find nothing to indicate it. Even after he hacked Marco's computer, he found nothing. He didn't know what to make of it, and before he could get in touch with Rocco about it, the FBI arrested him. All of it was too convenient.

Something wasn't adding up, and if he could figure it out, maybe he'd find a way out of his own personal hell. *I'll find a way back to you, Bianca. You have my word.*

Chapter Five

Days passed, and there seemed to be no progress made, making Bianca doubt her decision to come to Rocco. Maybe if she had taken the information straight to the police, things would have been different. She couldn't keep her thoughts from circling back to Anthony. Knowing he was locked in a cell with who knows what happening to him tightened her chest making it hard to breathe. She didn't care what it cost her personally. If she ever got her hands on Marco, she'd make him pay.

Everyone around her referred to him as Paxton but it was next to impossible for her to say that name. To her, he was Anthony. Calling him anything else felt as though she'd lose him completely. Unable to sever the irrational bond and use his birth name, she clung to the memory of their time together by calling him Anthony.

Rubbing her arms, she looked around the room. Rocco's penthouse was beginning to close in around her, but she was too afraid to leave. Thanks to Rocco, Gino had been arrested, but it was likely another one of Marco's men waited outside for her. Her brother wasn't the type of man to give up. Unlike their father who had kept her sheltered from his underworld life, Marco worked to prepare her for something. Every time he ordered her to an event at his house, he gave her a long list of instructions down to what she should wear. He wanted something from her, but what, she didn't know. Maybe he hoped to make her a wife of someone to ensure peace or more drug trade. She didn't know, but he never did anything without a motive.

"Bianca!" The urgency in Rocco's voice caused her to freeze in place for a split second.

She dropped the papers she held, rose from the sofa, and headed back to where Rocco worked. He had been working from his home office almost since the time she arrived. At first, she wondered if he was concerned about leaving her alone, but when she confronted him about it, he explained distractions were minimal when working there. Flash handled whatever needed to be done with Phantom Security, allowing Rocco and Elise to focus on Paxton.

As she expected, Rocco sat behind the antique desk carved with so much detail she couldn't take it all in. His black hair had rivets from him driving his fingers through it so many times during the day. His shoulders seemed relaxed yet the intense stare at the computer screen made her believe he found something.

"Bian—"

"I'm here." She waited until he looked up at her. "What's going on?"

"I got the wheels of justice spinning. They can be slow moving at times, but we're spinning them as fast as we can."

"What does that mean?" She strolled further into the office. "What kind of timeframe are we talking?"

"Bianca…" He got up from behind the desk and came around to stand in front of her. "I'm doing what I can. This would be simpler if he was pending trial, then we could get Paxton out on bail, but being convicted, he's already in the penitentiary. He's been there for weeks, and I have no idea how far Marco's influence reaches. This needs to be done carefully, or we put Paxton at risk."

"I want him out of there." She sank down into one of the plush burgundy chairs in front of the desk. "What must he think?"

"We're getting there." He reached forward and placed his hand on her shoulder. "Elise found proof Paxton has tried to contact us, but the calls are being rerouted. She's taken steps to correct the issues and assures me if he tries to call again, we'll receive it. Meanwhile I'm using one of my connections to try to get a message to Paxton."

"What do you mean a connection? If someone at the prison finds out we're trying to get him out he could be killed. Marco wants him dead."

"One of my employees has a brother who works there as a prison guard. I've spoken with him, and he'll do what he can, but Paxton's in solitary confinement for fighting. Word came down this morning he's to do thirty days."

"Thirty days!"

"He's been in and out of solitary since he arrived, each time he's been involved in a fight. There's talk they're going to move him to a different housing unit, taking him out of general population."

"He's protecting himself. Solitary means safety. Marco must be trying to have him killed in prison." She couldn't wrap her head around this. Rocco talked as if Anthony would still be there in thirty days. Would it take that long? There had to be another option. She hadn't been able to come up with anything yet, but it didn't mean there wasn't one. She'd read all about the hole when she researched what he'd be dealing with in prison. Round the clock lockdown in the cell, the only escape was an hour rec time, five days a week, and showers every three days. No human contact could drive someone insane. In her heart, she knew they wouldn't receive a call from him anytime soon. Solitary would mean the loss of his privileges. *Please, Anthony, stay strong. Don't give up.*

"Bianca?"

Blinking, she realized while she was lost in the horrors Anthony was going through, Rocco stood in front of her. "I'm sorry, what?"

"Are you okay?"

"Okay?" She chuckled. "I don't even know what that is anymore."

"Do you want me to get Elise? It might be easier for you to talk to her."

"No, let her work. I'll be fine. I should let you—" When she started to rise, he kept his hand firmly on her shoulder, forcing her to remain seated.

"I need to ask you a couple questions." When she relaxed back into the chair, he stepped around her to the chair beside her, pulling it closer. "Before Paxton went undercover I thought my team extensively investigated Marco Nitti, so that Paxton would have all the information he needed. Initially we found your father to have only one child, Marco, to his wife, Mrs. Nitti. It wasn't until Paxton went missing that I personally started digging through Marco, the organization, and eventually your father. Since he's deceased we hadn't looked extensively into your father, but when I did that's when I found you."

"Those were Father's wishes." Before meeting Rocco's gaze, she ran her hand down the arm of the chair, the soft suede material felt smooth along the skin of her palm. "We have different mothers. I am the product of an affair, one lasting more than ten years. When I was born, I was given my mother's last name for my protection. Though Marco says it was to protect his mother from the shame of knowing her husband was sleeping around on her. But how could she not know? He spent at least three nights a week at our house, the rest of the time he was at Marco's home. Those nights I was told he was working late. Even after the affair ended, he was there several days a week. He was always in my life. In middle school, I started to hear rumors he was in the mafia. When I questioned it, he made the decision to send me away to boarding school. He claimed they wanted me to have a better education. I understood public school was different from the boarding school where they sent me. No longer was I sitting around class bored because I already knew what was being taught. It wasn't until later I realized it was to keep his other life hidden from me."

"Your father went to great lengths to keep you hidden."

"A few days before he died, I had finally returned home after graduating from college. I had barely unpacked when he pulled me aside to explain what his so-called business was. He kept it hidden from me because he didn't want me to be involved in it. He encouraged me to open my own practice as I always dreamed, but I never got the chance. When he died, Marco took over, and for the last year, he's been shoving me into the world I never wanted anything to do with."

"Your own practice?"

"I'm a licensed psychologist," she explained. "Anthony and I talked about it. He encouraged me to put my foot down with Marco and follow my dreams, but that's easier said than done. Marco didn't want to hear about my 'stupid' college degree. I owed him because our father paid for my education. It was time for me to pay for my fancy degree."

"When this is over, I assure you we'll handle this in a manner that will leave you with the freedom to do whatever you want. Marco will no longer be an issue for you."

She tried not to read into his words because it left her with a knot in her stomach. Would he kill Marco? Death seemed like the only way her brother wouldn't be an issue for her. He wasn't the type to give up. This debt he believed she owed would be something he'd hold over her head for as long as he could. When he could no longer use her college education as leverage, he'd find something else. There was no escaping it as long as Marco was in power, and she was alive.

"I'd dress up and play the part for Marco if that's what it took to get Anthony out of prison. Starting my own practice would be a forgotten memory if it could save him. He means more to me than anything." Since middle school, she'd worked hard so one day she could open her practice and counsel at risk youth. There, she could make a difference, but she'd give it all up for his freedom. Even if it meant she had to allow Marco to control her life. She'd walk willingly into the world of darkness to save the one man who held her heart.

"Give me time. We'll get him back, and you can have the life you wanted. There's no reason you have to choose between anything." He placed his hand on hers, squeezing gently. "Trust me."

"I believe you'll do whatever you can to get him back, but that doesn't mean he won't still be in danger. Marco isn't a man to give up. He'll continue to go after Anthony, and as soon as he figures out why I came here, he'll come after you. He won't stop until everyone is dead."

His gaze shifted back to her face as he took her in again. "When you first arrived, I wasn't sure about you."

"What do you mean?"

"Marco could have sent you here to gain information for retaliation, but in the last few days, I've dug into your past enough to know your relationship with Marco is limited and rocky at best. If he were going to send someone here to infiltrate us, he'd use someone more convincing. Still, it wasn't enough for me to trust you. Elise on the other hand disagreed, she believed you were trustworthy from the start and she was right."

"What convinced you?"

"You did. When you spoke about Paxton, I could see the connection you had with him, but now, I realize there's more. You're in love with him." Rocco pulled his hand back from hers and reached across his desk, shuffling through a stack of papers before finding the one he wanted. "Early this morning, I received a package from an informant of mine. It seems Marco has made some enemies since taking over for your father."

"We all have enemies." Over the past year, she realized it was part of the life Marco was dragging her into. She could spend the rest of her life looking over her shoulder, waiting for someone to take a hit out on her, or she could live her life. She chose to live, while Marco chose to hide behind his crew. Yet another way they differed.

"With the Mexican cartel?" He held out the paper to her, and her hand shook as she reached out to take it. "He screwed the cartel out of almost two million dollars on a drug and weapons trade. They want him dead."

"Pieces…" Her throat tightened as she stared down at the information.

"He claims to have the highest kill count for the cartel, but he never leaves enough evidence for him to be charged. The only thing left of the bodies are pieces, hence the nickname. Marco has bigger things to worry about than Paxton."

Her gaze continued to scan down the printout in her hand until something else caught her attention. "Why is my name on here? I've done nothing." With each word, her voice rose.

He moved off the chair and squatted in front of her. "Bianca, look at me."

"Marco fucks up a deal, and I end up on some man's hit list."

"Pieces isn't after you. The cartel has your name as someone with possible information on Marco." He tossed the paper back onto the desk.

"That doesn't mean he won't come after me if they can't find Marco." Terror crept into every muscle of her body as she fought to keep control of her emotions. "I'll fucking kill Marco for this."

"I'm not going to let anything happen to you. You're safe here. We're dealing with this situation as well, but you need to do what I say. I know you feel cooped up, but it's keeping you safe. If you need to go somewhere, we can make arrangements, but you're not going anywhere alone."

"I'll do whatever you need me to do." She ran her hands along her thighs, wiping away the moisture that formed as she stressed over the new development. "You've been working around the clock, surely there's something I can do. Let me help. Please, Rocco. We're fighting for the same thing. If I can do something to speed up the process of getting Anthony out of prison then you have to let me."

"Actually, there is something." He reached back over his desk and grabbed a pad of paper that sat next to the laptop. "I've made a list of people who continue to come up on Marco's computer. I have a general idea about each of them, but I need you to help fill in the blanks."

"I don't know how much help I can be. Marco didn't confide in me. If anything, he considered me a pawn or a showpiece."

"Anything you can tell me will be helpful." He handed her the pad. "I want to have all the information laid out for Mayor Folger and the police to speed up the process of bringing Paxton home."

She held the pad in her hand but hadn't looked at the names yet. Her thoughts were too jumbled to focus. This felt a lot like betraying her father's memory, but he had been clear he hadn't wanted her involved in this lifestyle. He wouldn't admit he regretted the life he lived, but he wanted more for her. Marco didn't have the same attitude, and she couldn't count how many times he had told her: *You were born into this thing of ours, there's no escaping it. Family business. Do your part.*

"I'll do whatever I can."

Don't worry, Marco. I'll do my part…my part to bring you down.

Finally awake, the images from Paxton's nightmare danced through his mind. The worst, Bianca's lifeless body lay at Marco's feet as he taunted him. *You thought that was the end of it, but it's only the beginning. She's as guilty as you. She forfeited her life when she chose you over the bond of blood.*

Pacing his cell, he fought to remain silent. Unlike the others, he couldn't afford to scream or rant. He had to make it appear his confinement wasn't affecting him. Anyone could be listening, and if they realized this was getting to him, it would get back to Marco. Survival meant he had to appear tough, even when he was holding onto the last shred of his sanity by a frayed strand.

Thirty days. He wasn't sure how he'd survive that long in the hole. It had only been a handful, and he was already going crazy. No amount of working out or sleeping would help pass that many days. Seven days before had been a stretch for him, but he managed. This time, he wasn't sure he could survive it and keep his sanity intact.

The service hatch opened, delivering his meal, and he turned toward it. "Drink your milk, it's good for you."

He caught a glimpse of the guards' face, but didn't recognize him. Rather than telling him to fuck off, he silently grabbed his tray and sat down on the small concrete desk. Milk was the last thing he wanted. A nice cold beer or a shot of strong liquor would help ease the pain within his head. A strong cup a coffee might help him decide if he had any moves left.

As the plastic tray thumped against the concrete the small carton of milk tipped, revealing a folded piece of paper. With the service hatch closed and the guards away from his door, he grabbed the paper. He wasn't sure what to expect as he opened it, but what he saw gave him hope. *R.A. knows, working on it. B's there and safe. Hang tight.* There was no way to take the message other than positive. There was only one person he knew who could be B. Bianca. Knowing she was there with Rocco lifted a weight off his chest. He needed to make sure Marco never got his hands on her again because she wouldn't make it out alive. The nightmares of her death would come true before Paxton could do anything about it. Marco believed family should rank over everything, and the family business he was forcing her into should supersede everything.

Once he found out Paxton wasn't who he said he was, Bianca was dropped into the heat of things. She would have betrayed Marco even if she hadn't known Paxton's true identity. He was thankful Rocco made safety improvements to the house before he took up residency. The hidey-hole saved

43

Bianca's life, and there was nothing more important.

Barely touching the food, he read the note over and over again. Questions raced through his thoughts. What would happen next? Could Rocco find a way to convince the authorities he wasn't this Chris Weaver? How was he going to do that when his fingerprints matched Weaver's? There seemed to be a mountain of issues piling up against him. All he could do was hope it worked out and soon.

Chapter Six

After more than a week, they weren't any closer to getting Anthony released. Bianca didn't know what else to do, but as she dressed for the day, she couldn't help question their methods. It seemed impossibly slow and tedious before. Now, it was beyond that. As she opened the dresser drawer and her fingers brushed over his long sleeve steel blue shirt, she realized she couldn't take anymore.

"That's it! I'm going to confront Marco." Needing comfort, she pulled out the shirt and slipped it on. It was too big on her but it served its purpose by giving her the courage she needed.

Knuckles rapped against her door as Rocco called to her. "Bianca?"

"Come in." She pushed the sleeves up and turned to face the door.

"Good, you're up." He stood in the doorway grinning. "Paxton always loved that shirt."

"Yeah, I'm going…" Not wanting to offend him, she stumbled over her words. "Rocco, I'm sorry. I appreciate what you're trying to do, but…I've got to go back to Chicago. It might be the only way to save Anthony."

"Save him by getting yourself killed." The smile dropped from his lips as he moved further into her bedroom. "That's not going to help, and you know it."

"I can't take it." She pushed her hair away from her face and tucked it up into the clip. "He's been in solitary for almost two weeks. How can you be so

45

calm about all of this?"

"Because, Bianca, we're close." At the sound of Elise's voice, Bianca turned to find her standing in the doorway with Flash at her side.

"More like because he's never been in Paxton's position." Flash stepped past his wife. "El's right, we're close, but it doesn't mean I'm not thinking the same thing you are."

"I've got to confront Marco. I might be able to—"

"It's not going to work." Rocco cut her off. "The cartel got tired of waiting for Marco to show his face outside of his house. They've attacked his home. A bunch of his crew were killed in the attack. Those who weren't, including Marco, were arrested last night. Marco's injured but alive."

"I missed my opportunity." She leaned back against the dresser.

"My attorney should arrive in Chicago in less than an hour to meet with Marco. He's offering a deal. He'll make a statement confirming the evidence we've already acquired proving his involvement in locking Paxton up, or he'll face a long list of other charges, including first degree murder," Rocco explained.

"A lighter sentence, but then he'll be back on the streets. That's not going to protect Anthony." She couldn't believe Rocco's plans. Everything they worked for would be ruined after the police released Marco. Putting a hit out on Anthony and anyone else from Phantom Security wouldn't be enough; Marco would want to dish out his own personal revenge.

"No." Flash came to stand between her and Rocco. "The evidence gathered from Paxton's undercover operation and what you gave us on the laptop have not been translated into charges. Once that happens I can assure you Marco will spend the rest of his life behind bars."

"That doesn't mean there won't be someone else who steps into his position." Elise clarified. "But it should keep the two of you out of danger."

She agreed with Elise. The new Don most likely wouldn't give a shit about her or Anthony since they were no longer a threat to the organization. He had only been undercover to search for Mayor Folger's niece, and she never wanted to be part of the family. Finally, she could have her freedom, but before she could hope for that, she needed Marco to agree to the stipulations.

"I'm leaving for Chicago in…" Rocco glanced down at his watch. "Thirty minutes. Either you're on the plane with me, or you're not. If you're not, I expect you to keep your ass in this condo and do whatever Flash and Elise tell you to do."

"If I'm going?" She needed to know what he expected from her because she was definitely going.

"Then you follow every instruction I give you. No matter what. I'm not going to let you sacrifice yourself. We'll have him out of there by the end of the month even if I have to send a team in to storm the place and rescue him. He's one of mine, and I'm not going to leave him there to rot." Rocco turned on his heel and headed for the door. "The car's leaving in ten minutes. Grab your stuff if you're coming and let's go."

"If things go well, Paxton will be returning with you by the end of the trip." Elise shot her a bright smile. "Have faith. Rocco has connections deeper than anyone I know. He can pull this off."

"If not this trip, the end of the month. Only another eleven days." Sarcasm dripped from her words. She couldn't last another eleven days, and she had a feeling neither could Anthony.

She moved over to the dresser where his go-bag waited on the floor. She only had a few minutes to grab their stuff and meet Rocco in the living room. As she turned around to drop the bag on the bed before digging out the clothes from the drawer, she found Flash lingering near the door.

"Rocco won't give up until he accomplishes what he needs to." Flash glanced out the door to make sure no one was listening before turning back to her. "You need to make sure you're willing to do the same."

"What's that supposed to mean?" With the bag on the edge of the bed, she returned to the dresser, grabbing out their clothes from the top drawer before turning around to add them to the bag.

"Paxton is a warrior and prides himself on his strength, but prison changes people. He's been locked in a cell with little human contact most of his time inside, and until recently, he didn't know if you were alive or dead. He had no way to know if Marco found you or what he might have done to you. That affects a man. You need to be ready for the fact he might not be the same person that went in. If you love him like I believe you do, then you'll support him and give him time."

"Before I came here, I read about your story. You were arrested on murder charges. They thought you killed Chief Dalton, Elise's father."

"Yeah, but he was alive and well." Flash dragged a hand through his shaggy hair. "That wasn't what I meant though. I did my time in prison, and you can ask El, I'm different than I was. Knowing Paxton is there brought the memories to the forefront. I know what he's going through, and if he needs someone to talk to, I'm around. There's going to be things he can't share with you because he wants to protect you. You need to respect that. Pushing isn't going to get him to open up. He'll do so when he's ready."

"And I'll be there." With the last of their things in the bag, she stared down at the mixture of their belongings. Determination flooded through every cell of her body. No matter what happened she wasn't leaving Illinois without Anthony. *I'm coming for you.*

"Good." He stepped forward and handed her a business card. "This has both mine and El's cell numbers on it. If either of you need anything, call us."

"Thank you." She took the card and stuffed it into the back pocket of her jeans. "Do you really believe we'll get him out?"

Flash nodded. "With the progress we've made, we were close, but this development has changed things. Now, get packed. I assume from the shirt you have a few of Paxton's things, but if you need more of his things, I can get them. Trust me when I say he's going to want a hot shower and his own clothes."

"I've got a few things, and we shouldn't be there long." With a quick tug of the zipper, she was ready. She grabbed the bag off the bed and hefted it up onto her shoulder. "Thanks, Flash."

"Don't thank me. You're the one about to do all the hard work." He shot her a smile as she continued past him and out to the living room. "Oh, Bianca, Anthony is his middle name. Paxton Anthony Payne. Growing up most of his family called him Anthony. While he hid parts from you, he never outright lied to you."

She didn't care about his name. A name was just something to call him by. What she cared about was the man he was. She wanted to believe he was still the same man whether he was Paxton or Anthony. Only time would tell, and hopefully soon, she'd find out. Her heart pounded making the world around her spin for a moment. *I'm coming for you Anthony.*

Their flight had barely touched down in Chicago when Rocco received a phone call. Bianca paced the private jet waiting for some kind of hint as to what was happening. A good sibling might be concerned about her brother, but he barely crossed her thoughts with Anthony filling her mind. Being back in the city where they had met and fallen in love made her sentimental. She knew he wasn't in Chicago. He'd been transferred a few hours away, but she could feel him there. Everywhere she looked, she could see them, memories of them together danced through her thoughts.

"How about a drink?" Jac Armiger offered. "A stiff drink to help calm your nerves."

"Calm my nerves!"

49

Rising from his chair, he grabbed ahold of her arm. "Shh, I know you're scared, but freaking out isn't going to help matters. Whoever Rocco is on the phone with, it's important."

"I can't stand waiting around another moment. I have to do something."

"Good, then you can go with Jac to the hotel and get us settled." Rocco stood and slid his cell phone into the pocket of his dress slacks. "I have something I must attend to."

"What? You've got to be kidding me?" She pulled out of Jac's grip. "I didn't come here to sit around some hotel."

"Actually, you did." He grabbed his briefcase and signaled for the flight attendant to open the plane's door. "I brought you on this trip for Paxton's sake. Otherwise, you're a security issue. When it comes to you, I don't know where the remainder of Marco's crew stands, nor do we know if Pieces is now gunning for you. Unless you want me to have the pilot return to New York, you'll do what I say."

"Damn it, Rocco." Unwilling to back down, she stalked toward him. "I've proven to you I can be helpful. Don't close me out, not now."

"I'm not closing you out. I'm going to meet with Marco, and before you say it, no, you can't go. He wants to discuss what my attorney presented him with."

"Your presence there might turn the deal south," Jac reasoned. "Marco believes you betrayed him and the family. Seeing you there, working with us to get Paxton released will only make his resolve against it that much stronger."

"Surely, I can go without him even knowing."

"Do you really believe he wouldn't learn you're there?" Rocco pressed. "He had enough connections to be able to make a dead man disappear, swap out finger prints, and everything else he had to do in order to have Paxton sent to prison. Yet you doubt he'd find out you're at the police station? Come on, Bianca, you're smarter than that."

Not wanting to admit he was right, even though he was, she grabbed her bag and glanced back at Jac. "Let's go."

"No wonder Paxton fell for you. Beautiful and smart." Rocco smirked as he disembarked the plane. "Keep your head down and listen to Jac. Tanner's already at the hotel. You'll be safe there and enjoy the view."

"What's that supposed to mean?" She glanced back at Jac.

"Rocco likes to do things in style." Jac grabbed his own bag and headed for the stairs. "Let's roll."

When she had arrived at Phantom Security and became sequestered in Rocco's suite, she realized quickly he liked things his way. He didn't flaunt his money but his building was done in style, which only enhanced his penthouse condo. Everything was beautiful from the marble countertops to the art hanging on the wall. No doubt it was expensive, but he never made her feel as though she were in a museum where she had to walk on eggshells. Somehow, he merged it all together to make it feel like an inviting home.

"How did you end up working for Phantom Security?" She asked as Jac led the way to the car.

"Dalton...I mean Elise." He handed his bag to the chauffeur and climbed into the backseat, and she did the same. "We were in the FBI together, working with the same team. The team had her back as she dealt with Lewis. He's the one who tried to kill Chief Dalton and frame Flash. When she left, I left. It was time. Rocco offered me a better position, giving me more time with my daughter. Plus, Elise and I have always been close. We're good friends, and we work well together."

"How old is your daughter?"

"Three. She's the best thing in my life." His lips curled up into a bright smile. "Her mama's not too far behind either."

"Oh...I didn't..." She glanced down at his finger, and there was no wedding band.

"We're divorced." The smile slipped from his lips. "I can't blame her. We married our senior year of college. A few months later, I went into the FBI. Things were fine at first but once I started traveling things became strained. It took a while for her to get pregnant which added to our discord. When our daughter was born, she wanted me to give up the FBI, to find something where I'd be home, but I couldn't. By the time, my daughter was a year old my wife couldn't take it any longer. Now, things are a little different."

"But don't you travel as much?"

"There's still traveling, just not as much." He shifted to meet her gaze. "It's a different kind of life now, and I rarely miss a weekend with my daughter. When I do, she knows about it before hand, or if there is an emergency, I let her know. I don't know if we'll ever have what we had before, but we can at least be in the same room without fighting."

"Tomorrow's Friday, and you're here. You're going to miss the weekend with them because of me."

"No." His gaze met hers. "I drove out to Jersey last night and took them out to dinner. After we got back to the house, I explained to her what was going on, and while I couldn't give her all the details, she understood I needed to come. When this is over, I'm taking a couple days off. There's a cabin at the lake we used to go to all the time. I'm going to take them there for a few days."

"I hope you can work things out with her. Not only for your daughter's sake, because you sound like you really love her." She shot him a grin. "I'm a romantic."

It hadn't taken long for Anthony to realize she was a romantic. After the first thriller movie they watched, she ranted about how the couple should have had their happy-ever-after, and he teased her about it. There wasn't anything mean about it, and the next movie they watched together was a romance. He didn't enjoy it as much, but he watched it for her. That was the type of man he was. Would he still be content to cuddle on the sofa and watch a movie together? She couldn't help but think back on Flash's words. This unfortunate event likely changed him. *No matter what happens it won't change the fact I love him.*

Chapter Seven

It was the middle of the night when Rocco rushed into Bianca's room and ordered her to get dressed. After throwing on her jeans and Anthony's steel blue shirt, they climbed into his chauffeured town car and drove for hours. She had no idea where they were going, and all Rocco would tell her was to wait and see. The early morning hours would soon bring dawn, and she had barely slept. Frustrated beyond words, she pulled her hair into a messy ponytail and leaned back against the seat. She wanted answers. Instead, she received the silent treatment from Rocco. By the time the car came to a stop, she was ready to scream.

"I need you to trust me." With his hand resting on the door handle, Rocco watched her. "Stay in this car, do not look out the windows. Be patient, and wait."

"Rocco, what's going on?"

"Do as I say, and you'll understand in a few minutes."

"Damn it, Rocco." She brought her leg up onto the seat and turned to face him. "You woke me up in the middle of the night to drive to who knows where, and the whole time, you've been on your computer or the phone. I'm exhausted, and I want some answers."

"I know, and if you're patient for five more minutes, you'll have them." He pushed opened the door and stepped out before quickly shutting the door behind him.

Temptation to move over to his side and peek out the window gnawed at her. What could a little peek hurt? Instead of giving into the allure, she forced herself to stay rooted in place. Whatever he was hiding had to be important; otherwise, he wouldn't have gone to such an extent. They were no longer in Chicago, but she had no doubt Marco's reach could find her wherever they were if he wanted to. Did this have something to do with that?

Anxiety built with every minute that ticked by until she wanted to scream. Unable to take it any longer but knowing the risks could outweigh the benefits; she forced herself to lean back against the soft leather. She closed her eyes and tried the deep breathing exercises Anthony had taught her to help her relax. Whatever reason Rocco brought her out in the middle of the night must be important. She trusted him this long; she needed to continue to trust him.

The car door opened, but she didn't bother to open her eyes. "Asshole, that was more than five minutes." The seat shifted as he climbed in to sit next to her, still she didn't open her eyes. "Can we go now? I'm exhausted."

"We can go anywhere you want to go, Bianca." The voice was different, smooth with a hint of southern drawl.

Squeezing her eyes shut, she tried to cling to his words. "Please, don't let me wake up."

"Darling, you're not asleep." Fingers caressed over her jaw, teasing up the curve of her cheek before making its way into her hair. "Open your eyes."

She didn't remember falling asleep, but she had been exhausted. If she opened her eyes, she knew she'd find herself alone in the back of the car. A dream was the only logical way he'd be there. Still his touch felt real against her heated skin. Temptation bubbled within her making it hard for her to keep her eyes shut.

"Bianca." Her name was barely above a whisper as he moved closer, his body brushing along hers. "Open your eyes."

"I don't want this to end." Before she could stop it, a single tear rolled down her cheek.

"Darling, it won't."

Against her better judgment, she opened her eyes. Anthony sat next to her. His short brown hair spiked every which way, and stubble along his jaw from a couple days without shaving made her want to reach out and touch him. Wearing his slim framed glasses that to her always made him sexier. It seemed too close to a dream. Still, she sat there frozen in place with her mouth slightly open as she stared into his hazel eyes. Part of her searched for something, anything to tell her he was the same man, while the other part was too shocked to move.

"Anth...Pax...I can't believe it's you." Seeing him there in front of her she realized that holding onto the name Anthony was childish. It didn't matter his name as long as he was still the same man who had stolen her heart.

"Come here, darling." Before she could move, he pulled her into his lap. "I can't believe this is actually happening. I can't believe you're here."

As the car accelerated forward, she wrapped her arms around his neck, pressing herself tighter against him. "Me either."

"Baby, I know you have questions, and I'm sure your pissed I lied to you—"

"We'll get through it." Not completely sure it wasn't a dream; she tightened her embrace around him. "What matters is you're here."

"You're right. We'll deal with it later. But there's one thing that can't wait. Before, when you said my name...baby, call me whatever you want. Anthony, Paxton, I don't care, as long as you're by my side. Just don't call me Chris Weaver. I was never him. You know that, don't you?" His hand slid along her back as he held her against him.

"I know." She whispered. "I've been worried you'd be different, but you're still my man. Whether you go by Anthony or Paxton, you're still the same person I fell in love with." Maybe it was the emotions of being reunited, but she believed they'd find a way to make this work. There would be aspects of him that were different. The biggest being his job. He no longer lived a life in the shadows; instead, he had an upstanding position. She wondered if he could accept where she came from and what connections to the darkness of Chicago she would always have.

"I never meant to lie to you."

"Let's not talk about it now." Bringing her arm down from where she wrapped around his neck, she placed her hand on his chest so she could feel his heartbeat against her fingers.

"What are you doing?" He asked when she kept her hand there.

"Your heartbeat…" She glanced back up at him. "Whenever I'd dream of you, I couldn't feel it. Now…I can't believe you're here. Rocco never said anything. I didn't know."

"Me either." He tangled his fingers in her hair and brought her head to rest against his chest. "Two weeks…maybe more…time runs together in there. I received the message that Rocco knew where I was and you were there, safe. Then nothing until tonight, I was pulled from the hole and ordered to dress. Without explanation, a few minutes later, I was forced out the back door."

"I'm so glad you're here." Yawning, she snuggled against him.

"Rest, darling, I'm not going anywhere."

"Let me get off you—"

"Not a chance." He held onto her tight. "I want you right here in my arms."

She relaxed against him and tried to let her mind go blank. She didn't want to think about where he had been or the hell they'd been through. All she wanted was to put the whole thing behind her. After everything they went through to drive them apart, spending the rest of her life with him felt right.

Freedom. Paxton cracked the window, allowing himself a breath of fresh air. The breeze was like a breath of air to a drowning man. He never valued it before, always took for granted it would always be there, but after the last couple of months of being confined to a small cell, he cherished his freedom. The first breath of air outside the prison walls was pure ecstasy. He would rather die than go back to where he'd come from.

If this was a dream, he wasn't going to give it up. As Bianca fell asleep in his arms, he clung to her, horrified even to close his eyes for fear she'd disappear and he'd be back in his musty cell. For weeks, he feared she might be dead, and even after he found out she was with Rocco, he wasn't sure he'd ever have her in his arms again. He'd thought his undercover stint made him lose her, but there she was, curled up in his embrace, sleeping peacefully.

The window between the driver and the back portion of the car lowered and Rocco turned in the passenger seat to glance back at them. "You should have told me about her."

"Why? So you could pull me out? Fuck that. I was close." He glanced down at her before returning his gaze back to Rocco. "I wasn't going to have you pull me out. I'd have been forced to leave her behind or tell you to fuck off. My job means a lot to me but not more than her. Fire me if you want, but I wasn't leaving her to deal with Marco's insanity. Do you have any idea what he planned for her?" The last part came out as more of a growl as he fought to keep his voice low.

"Yeah, I found the emails on the laptop."

"Laptop?"

Rocco tipped his head toward Bianca. "Your girl there is smart. She grabbed your go-bag and your laptop before she took off. It took her a couple weeks to come to us, but when she did, it allowed us to put the pieces together. We had no idea you were in there under another name."

"I tried to make contact."

"I know. Marco had people inside, blocking any attempt. By the time, we found out you had already gotten yourself sent to segregation."

"Got myself sent there!" His hands clenched as anger boiled within him. "You make it sound like it was a luxury. Do you think I wanted to be there?"

"That's not what I meant, and you know it." Rocco eyed him. "You're pissed because of where you've been, but we're doing what we can to take care of Marco and keep both of you safe."

The driver said something to Rocco, but Paxton couldn't make it out. "Make a right, and I'll let the pilot know to redirect to our standby point."

"What's going on?"

"There's an accident blocking the interstate. We're going to meet the helicopter at a secondary point." Rocco explained, his fingers tapped over his phone, obviously alerting the pilot to the situation.

"Then what?"

"Take the helicopter back to Chicago to our waiting plane and on to New York." Rocco glanced back at him. "I'm sure you'd rather shower and change first, but you can do it on the plane. We need to get Bianca out of the city to keep her safe. Once Marco finds out he has additional charges being added, he's going to be outraged."

"I heard through the prison grapevine the cartel put a hit out on him. Is she in danger?"

With a raised eyebrow, Rocco met Paxton's glance. "We're all in danger if shit hits the fan."

"What can I do?" He caressed his hand along her back. After almost losing her once, he'd be damned if he was going to allow it to happen now. He'd protect her from whatever the cartel or Marco's crew through at them.

"Keep your head down, and focus on Bianca. She's been strong through all of this, but thinking she lost you messed with her head."

He didn't doubt it threw her off balance; it did the same thing to him. The idea he failed to protect her made him think things he never thought before. He wanted Marco dead, but before he killed the bastard, he wanted him to suffer. Lock him up in a tiny cell with little to no human contact for days on end and see how long it took for his mind to snap. Marco had no idea locking Paxton up would only make him more determined to seek revenge. As soon as he could figure out how, he was going to have a little fun with that asshole before he killed him, unless someone else got to Marco first.

"Don't focus on revenge, focus on your girl."

"My attention span can handle both." He didn't have to look up at Rocco to know his boss wasn't happy with the comment, but after what Marco put Bianca through, it was worth Rocco being upset.

"Listen to me, Paxton. I'll handle him."

Before Paxton could argue the car came to a stop, and Rocco climbed out. When Paxton's door opened, he slid out of the car, carrying Bianca so as not to wake her. Slowly, he made his way to the helicopter, only to find Jac and Tanner standing by waiting for them.

"Man it's good to have you back." Jac placed a hand on his shoulder and squeezed. "Your girl has been worried about you."

"So I learned. Let's get her out of here." He climbed into the helicopter and settled in, just as Bianca began to stir. "Shh, baby, go back to sleep." He pressed his lips to her forehead and breathed in the scent of her.

Less than two hours later Paxton was back in New York City stepping off the elevator with his go-bag in one hand and his arm wrapped around Bianca's waist. The night had been long for both of them. Taking a hot shower and getting some rest were at the top of his agenda. "Come on, darling."

"Where are we going?"

"My place." He slipped his arm from her waist so he could unlock the door and glanced around the empty hallway. There were only four other condos on this floor, and the last he was aware, two housed Phantom Security agents out on assignment and the other one was vacant. Still, he had to be sure no one was nearby. "If you'd prefer to stay with Rocco, I'm sure he won't mind."

"Is that what you want? For me to stay with Rocco?" She refused to meet his gaze, but there was a hint of sadness in her tone.

"Fuck no, Bianca." He pushed her inside and slammed the door shut behind them. "I want you with me. To have you a couple floors up in his bed pisses me off. You're mine."

"I was never in his bed."

"Darling, you know what I mean." He pressed her against the wall and dropped the bag at their feet. "Do you have any idea what it does to me to see you standing there in my shirt?"

"I…um…" She glanced down at the shirt as if she forgot she was wearing it and tears sprang to her eyes. "I just missed you so much."

"There's no need to explain." He cupped the sides of her face. "You're beautiful in everything you wear, fucking stunning naked, but seeing you wearing my shirt does something to me. It makes me so fucking hot." He pressed his lips to hers, claiming her mouth with his own. Her lips opened willingly, allowing his tongue to slip into her mouth. With every kiss, the need for her grew stronger.

When the kiss ended, her fingers wrapped around his shirt, and she tried to catch her breath. "I'd rather have you naked."

"Hmm…" He lifted her up, giving her no choice but to wrap her legs around his waist. "I think we can arrange that." With her wrapped around the front of him, he strolled toward the master bedroom. "I want to shower. Join me?"

"I figured you'd do that on the plane. I had your things in the bag."

"So thoughtful." He dropped her down onto the edge of the bed. "I couldn't separate myself from you even for a short shower. Plus, five minutes of hot water wasn't going to be enough to make me feel any better."

"Why don't you go get in, and I'll join you in a few minutes. I'm sure…"

"What's wrong?"

"Nothing." She tried to give him a bright smile, but it fell flat, letting him know something was up.

"Bianca?" He used his forefinger to tip her head back, forcing her to look up at him.

"Something Flash said." She shrugged. "I thought maybe you'd want to shower alone."

"That's the last thing I want right now. I can't even fathom allowing you out of my sight." He grabbed hold of the bottom of his shirt and pulled it up and over her head. "Trust me."

"There's no one I trust more." She rose to stand before him and unhooked her jeans. "Am I going to have to tear your clothes off you, or are you going to join me?"

In a blink of an eye, they stripped out of their clothes, and he pressed her naked body along the front of his. "You're even more beautiful than I remember."

"Funny I was thinking something similar." Her hands roamed over his chiseled chest and down the tight muscles of his arms. "You've bulked up."

"Nothing else to do besides work out and fantasize about you. Sleep only led to unwanted dreams." Even though he didn't say it, half of his dreams about her had been as unwanted as his nightmares. He could practically see her dead, and there was nothing he could do to stop it. Every move he made always ended up in the same way. Seeing her lying dead at Marco's feet made him want to tear that bastards throat out with his bare hands. *Soon. Run, Marco, I'm coming for you. Fucking rat bastard.*

Chapter Eight

Locked in his embrace, Bianca stood at Paxton's side as he fiddled with the water temperature. Her hands roamed over his body, taking in the new muscle, while her gaze stayed focused on his face. To be there with him was like a dream come true, and as long as she held on to him, it wouldn't end. She'd spend her life right there with him, holding on for dear life, if that's what it took. She didn't believe any of this was a dream, but if it was, she wasn't about to let it go. She'd stay right there with him for as long as she could. For her, he was it, the one person she wanted to spend her life with.

Her arm brushed along the cool glass shower door, causing her to shiver, and he turned toward her. "Ready?"

"Always ready when it comes to you." Steam rose from the stall as he pulled her with him into the cascade of water.

Hot water flowed down her body, nearly scalding her. "Now I know what a lobster goes through."

"Too hot?" He shifted his body in front of hers, allowing his back to catch most of the spray. "Let me turn it down."

"No, leave it." She stopped him as he reached back for the handle. "Kiss me."

Not having to be asked again, his lips crushed against hers with such force she'd have stumbled if he hadn't wrapped his arms around her waist. Full of promise and desire, the kiss made her sink into his embrace. It wasn't that she wanted this because they had been separated for so long, it had always been like that between them. Though their relationship was full of heat and desire from the beginning, there was more between them.

His tongue invaded her mouth. She was met with the spiciness of coffee he downed on the plane. Before her thoughts could turn to anything else, his hands ran down her body, exploring her curves. Slowly, he worked along her skin before sliding his hand between her legs. As his finger caressed her clit, sending waves of pleasure through her, she couldn't stop the moan from escaping around his unrelenting kiss. He worked his fingers inside of her, as his thumb continued to tease along her clit, pleasuring her in ways she only imaged. Breaking the kiss, he pulled his hand away and lifted her off the ground. He pressed her back against the cool tiles and kissed along her neck. "So fucking beautiful."

Wrapping her legs around him, she let her hands roam over his back. His shaft teased along her most intimate parts making her grind down against him. While he always made foreplay worth it for her, she wanted him inside of her. Teasing her nails along his back, she arched into him as he sucked her nipple between his lips, gently tugging until a moan tore from her lips. "Please…I want you. Now."

"Darling…" He let her nipple slip from his lips and rose so his face was inches from hers. "You've always had me. *Always.*"

The way his fingers dug into her hips and his eyes stared into hers, she realized there was more to his comment than she understood, but before she could question it, he distracted her. Sliding his shaft along her folds, he teased along her opening before he slipped his hand between them. Readjusting, he thrust inside her with one continuous motion. Her head tipped back as another moan tore from her.

Buried to the hilt inside of her, he paused and pressed her tight against the wall. "The thought of being deep inside of you like this kept me going. I love the way the green comes out in your hazel eyes when you're turned on and the way your body reacts to mine with the simplest touch."

Any shred of reservation she had about what would happen between them disappeared as she brought her hand from his back to cup the side of his face. "I love you, Paxton."

With his eyes closed, he tipped his head forward, pressing his forehead against hers.

"Baby?" With one hand on his cheek, she brought her other one up to push his dark brown hair away from his face.

"Say it, again." His voice was strained with emotion.

"I love you."

"No, the other part."

She pressed her lips to his in a quick kiss. "Paxton. I love you, Paxton."

"Fuck, darling!" His eyelids sprang open, and their gazes locked. "I love the way you say my name, but I was serious earlier. I don't care what you call me as long as you're in my arms."

"There's nowhere else I'd rather be."

Slowly his hips pumped against her, working his shaft in and out of her. With each pump, his pace sped until she arched into him, matching his thrusts with her own. With her fingers still tangled in his hair, she kept his face close, watching his eyes as he drove into her.

"Don't stop." She tipped her head back, letting it rest against the tiled wall of the glass-enclosed shower as her ecstasy grew. His own grunts kept pace with her moans. "Oh, Paxton!"

He grabbed hold of her hips and drove his shaft into her harder and faster. The frenzy had her moaning until she called out his name and groaned as her climax sent her over the edge. He followed her moments later as he buried himself deep within her one final time.

"Fuck, darling" He dipped his head to her neck, planting soft kisses along the curve before working his way up to her ear. "That was too quick. I'm sorry."

"Don't." She pressed her finger to his lips. "We needed that, and who said we were done. We'll finish this shower and who knows. A little sleep, some more lovemaking. We've got the rest of our lives."

Sun streamed through the curtains, giving Bianca enough light in the otherwise dim room to see Paxton's face as she lay there watching him. She should have been sleeping, exhaustion clung to every muscle, but she was too afraid when she woke up he'd be gone. More than that, she was still trying to work out her own thoughts.

Sometime since they'd been reunited, he went from Anthony to Paxton. Before she resisted calling him anything other than Anthony. Partially she believed calling him Paxton she'd lose the man she fell in love with. The other part was she was scared of what Paxton would be like. All she could picture in her mind was a man with split personalities, but it wasn't anything like what she encountered. Whether he went by Anthony or Paxton, he was still her man. She loved him. While they were sure to have some bumps in the road ahead of them, she wanted them to make it. He meant everything to her, and the thought of losing him again tore her heart apart.

"No! You can't have her!" Paxton screamed in his sleep.

"Baby." She snuggled closer to him and placed her hand on the side of his face.

"Stay the fuck away from her, or I'll kill you!" Anger seeped from his words, and the muscles in his arms tightened.

"Paxton, baby, wake up." She wasn't sure how to pull him from his nightmare. He had never been one to have nightmares, and as a light sleeper, she had been able to wake him easily. Not this time. Nudging him gently his eyes sprang open. "Are you okay?"

"Fuck!" He wrapped his arms around her, pulling her tight against his body. "You're here."

"Where else would I be?" She tried to make light of it, but as he clung to her, it was clear something was going on.

"I'm sorry, darling."

With her chest pressed up against his, she looped her arm around his back, trying to ease his shivers. "Are you okay?"

"Fine."

"Don't..." She pulled back from him. Suddenly, it was too much, and something snapped within her.

"What?"

"Don't lie to me." She snapped. "After everything don't you think I deserve at least that?"

"Bianca—" He reached for her, but she pulled further away.

"You lied to me." She dragged her hand through her hair. "I know you had your reasons, and I accepted them, but I can't..."

"I'm sorry, Bianca." His hand caressed along her arm, and she didn't pull away. "I know I fucked up, but I'm going to spend the rest of my life making it up to you if you'll let me."

"I shouldn't have snapped. It was...damn it, I know you're not okay. I can't help if you lie to me about it."

"Just being here beside me, you're helping." He tugged lightly on her arm. "Come back here, please."

"Tell me what you were dreaming about. Who were you screaming at? Who wanted her? Who were you protecting?" The questions rattled off so quickly she wasn't sure he caught them all. "Give me something."

"You...I was trying to protect you." Letting out a deep breath, he collapsed back against the pillows.

"From what?" She scooted closer so she sat next to him, looking down at him.

"Forget it."

"No." She placed her hand on his chest over his heart. "We've both gone through hell lately, and I get there's things you won't want to talk to me about, but shutting me out isn't the answer, either. If you won't talk to me, talk to Flash. He'll understand."

"Understand what?" His gaze focused back on her, making her shift uneasily.

"Whatever happened in…" She stumbled over the word, not wanting to say it. "Prison."

"Fuck that." He rose onto his elbow, and his fingers caressed along her thigh. "After I was arrested, one of Marco's contacts came to me. He warned me Marco was going after you. Desperately, I tried to get to you, to find some way of getting word to you, or to Rocco, and I failed. A week later word traveled around that you were dead. Every night, I've lived through the dreams of failing to protect you. Bianca, I never regretted getting involved with you, but everyday I've regretted leaving you in that situation. I should have told you the truth and got you out of there. I knew Marco was sniffing around me. I never suspected he learned anything."

"Nothing happened. I'm safe." She placed her hand over his. "We all have regrets. I've hated myself since that night. I should have come out and told them you weren't Chris Weaver. Maybe you'd have never been arrested."

"No, darling, we'd have been killed instead. Gino waited outside. You did the right thing staying hidden." He grabbed hold of her wrist and pulled her down to lie next to him. "You mean everything to me, and I'd spend the rest of my life behind bars if it meant keeping you safe."

"Paxton…" She tipped her head to look at him. "Don't do anything stupid. I'm safe right here with you."

"Nothing stupid, but calculated revenge is another thing."

"I can't lose you…not again." She looped her arm over his chest and pressed her body against his. "You're all I have…all I want."

"Being behind bars isn't going to stop Marco. Even when someone else steps into his position, there will still be those loyal to him and your father. They'll carry out whatever orders he hands out."

Lovers are not as important as family. Do not confuse his devotion with the bond of blood. In her mind, she could picture Marco standing in front of her as he said those words. "Bond of blood…"

"What?" Paxton's hand stopped sliding along the length of her back.

"He wasn't talking about blood of biological family but the bond of his crew. Father always said they were bonded closer than family."

"She's as guilty as you. She forfeited her life when she chose you over the bond of the family. That's a direct quote from Marco's puppet." His arm tightened around her for a moment, as if he was afraid of what would happen. "Rocco won this round by getting me out, and Marco put behind bars, but you have to realize it's not over. If we don't make the first move, it leaves us open for whatever plan of action he puts into play. I refuse to allow that to happen. It's my duty to protect you, and that's what I'm going to do."

"By risking yourself?" She shook her head. "There's got to be another way."

"We'll talk to Rocco about it. For today, let's enjoy each other." He pressed his hand to her back, holding her close. "I have a lot to make up for, both with mistakes and time missed."

"Time missed maybe, but mistakes…we both made our share of those. We'll get through them, and you know what, we'll be stronger for it." Resting her shoulder in the crook of his arm, she snuggled against him. "Like you said, we have the rest of our lives."

Chapter Nine

Glancing at the bedside clock Paxton realized they must have dozed off again. It was now just before eleven in the morning, and Bianca still snuggled against him, sleeping peacefully. He pressed his face against the top of her head, breathing in the sweet vanilla scent of her shampoo. He lied to her about who he was and had worked to take down her brother, yet she was still there by his side. He was sure there were going to be bumps in the future for them but as long as they stuck together everything would turn out okay in the end.

"Did you get any sleep?" She leaned back into him, and he caught sight of the Phantom Security logo on the pocket of his shirt, which she wore.

"Some." He slid his hand along her back. "You?"

"I haven't slept this well since…"

When he realized she couldn't bring herself to say it, he squeezed her tight against him. "I know, darling. It's all over now."

"Make me forget." She tipped her head up to look at him. "Even if just for a little while."

"I can do that."

"Really? How?" She raised an eyebrow at him, tempting him.

"I have my ways." He took hold of her hand and slid it down his body, allowing her fingers to tease over his hard manhood as it strained against his boxers. "I told you before you do something to me when you're wearing my shirt."

"Really now? Maybe I'll have to take to wearing them all the time."

"As much as I like you in them, I love you naked more. How about you wear nothing at all?" He grabbed hold of the edge of the shirt and pulled it up her body.

Helping, she rose onto her knees and pulled the shirt off, revealing her naked body. Before he had a chance to enjoy the sight, wrap his arms around her, and bring her back down to him, she slipped lower on the bed, pushing the covers back as she went. "What are you doing?"

"Nothing." She bit the corner of her lip, giving him a nervous smile. Her hand slipped under the waistband of his boxers, gently lifting the material away. He arched his hips allowing her to slip them down. As he kicked the boxers off, she slipped between his legs, forcing him to spread them.

"Bianca…"

"Let me do this." She wrapped her hand around his length. Before he could argue, she knelt and wrapped her mouth around his cock.

"Bianca…" A groan escaped his lips as she took him deep enough that he felt her throat constrict around him. Not deep enough to meet the end but as far as she could go. Her hand wrapped around the rest, applying enough pressure to have him groaning. "Your mouth around my hard dick is fucking amazing, but I want to be inside you. I want you to scream my name."

"I haven't screamed your name enough?" She teased, still holding his shaft in her hand, her long dark brown hair flowing around her almost like a veil.

"I'll never get tired of hearing you say my name." He wrapped his hand around her bicep and pulled her up toward him. As she came up, he leaned forward. His arms wrapped around her waist drawing her closer as he kissed her. Unlike before when their kisses were full of need this one was slow and deliberate. He wanted the kiss to show her the love he had for her.

"You mean so much to me." He slid his hands down her body. "So fucking beautiful."

"One thing to another, I love how your brain works," she teased.

Ignoring her little dig, he pressed his lips to hers as he cupped her breasts. Teasing her nipples between his fingers as he gently swirled his thumb against the hard buds before pinching them slightly. Moaning softly against his lips she arched into his touch. He abandoned her mouth and kissed her neck, nibbling down her jawline to her shoulder. Slowly, he teased kisses down her chest until he came to her breast and flicked his tongue over her hardened nipple. With every caress, her body vibrated against his, as he fanned the flames of their desire. Loving how her body reacted to him, he sucked a nipple into his mouth, allowing his teeth to drag round the hardened bud.

"This is what I missed the most."

"What, me naked?" she teased.

"Well, that, too." His hand slid to the small of her back. "The way your body responds to me. You were made for me."

"Hmm, I thought you were the one made for me."

"How about we were made for each other?" With that, he rolled her over so she was on her back, and he was hovering over her. His hands slid over her body, teasing down her sides before caressing over her hips. "I'm never letting you go."

"Fine by me. There's nowhere I'd rather be than right here with you."

Taking her words as an invitation, he trailed his hand over her hip and between her thighs. His caress had her spreading her legs, giving him the access he needed. Ever so slowly, he teased his fingers along her inner thigh until he slipped his finger between her folds, quickly finding her core and working deep inside her. His thumb brushed along her clit, sending her wiggling against his hand.

"You're wet and ready. I thought I'd have my work cut out for me." She arched into him as he worked his fingers in and out of her, each pump of his hand growing quicker and quicker. Her back arched, and he shook his head. "Not yet, darling."

"Paxton." She moaned in desperation as he moved his hand away from her. "I need this."

"Oh, I know, sugar, and I'll give you what you need. You've got to be patient."

"When have you ever known me to be patient?" She bitched, as her hand slipped between them before she reached for his cock.

Before she could wrap her hand around his dick, he grabbed hold of her wrists and pulled them together, forcing them over her head. "No, I'm setting the pace today. You'll have to wait until I'm good and ready."

"Paxton! Please, baby…"

Ignoring her pleas, he trailed a blaze of kisses down her body, while his free hand strolled along the curves of her side. Just light enough to tickle. With every touch, she arched her hips into him, demanding more. "You're so damn sexy when you're impatient."

"You better be glad I love you because this is torture. Pure torture."

"You haven't seen anything yet, Bianca." His thumb brushed along her clit, and her hips lifted off the bed, arching against him. "You keep that up, and I'll stop."

"It's been so long."

"Less than twenty-four hours." He smirked at her, pulling his hand away.

Shocked by the loss of his touch, she opened her eyes, only to find him grinning down at her. "Are you trying to draw this out, so I'll roll you onto your back and have my way with you? Because I will."

"I'd love for you to try. But no, I was about to make my move. Maybe I should wait a bit longer. Draw out the torture a bit more." As she fought to release her hands from his grasp, he leaned down, pressing his face against the curve of her shoulder until his mouth was next to her ear. "You might have trouble, rolling me over when you don't have the use of your hands."

Her legs wrapped around him, but that only brought her pussy closer to his cock, making her freeze mid-motion.

"How's that working for you?" He nipped her earlobe, sucking it between his teeth.

"Paxton." Her voice barely above a whisper as she begged.

He let go of her ear and leaned back up so he looked down at her. "You're so fucking sexy when you're begging. Maybe I'll give into you and fuck you until you can't stand."

"Then stop making me beg for it." She unwrapped her legs, letting them rest on either side of him. "Let my hands go. I want to run them over your body."

He let go of her wrists and placed his hands on either side of her, using them to brace himself. He teased the tip of his dick along her slit before arching forward, shoving into her pussy with one quick movement. A moan echoed through the room as her core muscles stretched to accommodate his width. "Oh!" The single word was breathless as she ran her hands up his chest.

Staring down at her, he slowly pumped his hips, sliding his dick in and out of her core. Using one arm to keep himself leveraged above her, he brought his other hand to her breast. He groaned as his fingers found her nipples. Rolling the hardened bud between his fingers, pinching it with enough pressure to have her arching forward, he increased his pace. Each pump of his hips had him going harder and faster, stealing her breath as her climax neared. Heat coiled between her thighs, and her sex clenched around him.

"Faster!" She lifted her body up to meet his.

"I love how fucking good you feel wrapped around my dick. So tight and wet." He pulled nearly his full length out, before slamming back into her. When he did, he sped his pace up. Their bodies rocked back and forth, each thrust gaining momentum, drawing him closer to the edge.

Letting go of her nipple, he slipped his hand between them, instantly finding her clit. His thumb brushed over the hardened bud. Sucking her lip between her teeth, she bit down, and he almost lost it. "Shit that's sexy."

Her legs wrapped around him, with her ankles locked together at the small of his back as he pounded into her faster. He wasn't sure if it was to keep him from pulling back too far or to keep him inside of her. Either way, he loved the way it felt. Tension had her muscles constricting around him as her orgasm neared, urging him to an even faster rhythm, and his eyes glazed over with his own ecstasy creeping up on him.

"Paxton." She moaned as her pussy walls tightened around him, and her climax sent him over the edge.

With her core muscles tightening around his dick, he was a goner. He slammed his dick deep within her for the final time and allowed himself to follow her over the edge into bliss. Leaning forward he pressed his forehead against hers and let go. Their gazes locked onto each other, as her nails raked down his sides, and she arched into him. Their moans echoed together until she collapsed back onto the bed. "Fuck, Bianca."

"That was even better than last night."

"Tell me about it." His voice was rough as he dipped his head into the curve of her neck. "You're so damn sexy when you're about to come. I love the way you pull your lip between your teeth. I swear that does it to me every time."

"Really now?" She arched an eyebrow. "I'll have to remember that."

"I have no doubt you will." He let out a light chuckle as he slipped out of her and collapsed next to her on the bed before pulling her snug against his body.

Resting her head in the crook of his arm, she let her fingers trail over his chest.

"What's wrong?" He asked as her expression changed from relaxed to something more serious.

"Before, you were toned, and I loved dragging my fingers along your rock-hard abs. Now, it's so much more. I love it, but at the same time, I hate it. I feel so safe in your arms, but then I remember how you bulked up, and I want to scream. I hate Marco for what he's done to you."

He reached up and placed his hand over hers. "Don't think about it. The past is what it is. We can't change it. What we can do is build a better and brighter future together."

Together. He wanted her as his wife, forever next to him.

Chapter Ten

By the time Paxton made it to Phantom Security's floor, he was fuming. Everything hit him at once as he strolled past his office and coworkers. This is where he was supposed to be. Now, he realized the undercover mission was something he never should have done. Yet without it, he wouldn't have found Bianca.

The door to Rocco's office was open, welcoming him. His boss sat behind his desk with his phone cradled between his shoulder and ear as he finished the phone conversation. "Let me know what you find." Without another word, he ended the call, placed the phone back in its cradle, and looked up at Paxton. "Have a seat."

"What the fuck happened? I waited for you for months!" Unable to keep the anger pent up any longer, it flowed freely through him.

"Calm down."

"Calm down?" He slammed his hands down on Rocco's desk, hard enough to move papers. "Do you have any idea what I went through for months? Every day the possibility of you setting things right and getting me out of there diminished. Would you have left me there to rot if it hadn't been for Bianca?"

"Paxton…" A female voice called from behind, but he wouldn't take his gaze off Rocco. The door clicked shut, and the woman neared. "I understand your frustration."

"Elise." His voice softened as he tipped his head toward her. "This is between Rocco and me."

"No, it's between all of us. Rocco, Flash, you, and me, we sat down and made the decision to allow you to go undercover. The consequences are something we all must deal with." She reached out and placed her hand over his. "We went over everything and never expected Mayor Folger to double cross us. His niece was never in any danger."

"I never found any evidence there was any sex trafficking going on." Paxton growled. "The whole operation was a lie."

"Elise went through the laptop and every communication with Marco, there was nothing. I don't believe he was ever involved in it. Drugs, gun, black market items, sure, but not women. He was a womanizer; he wanted to keep them for himself. He hadn't met a woman he didn't want to get into bed. He wouldn't have been able to separate himself from the job," Rocco explained.

"That doesn't explain why it took you months to find me. Were you going to leave me there to rot?"

"After you missed your check in we knew something had happened, but we had no idea you were in prison. You were there when I set up pings on your name and for Anthony Davis. We never got a single hit." Elise shifted slightly. "We thought…"

"What?"

"We thought you were dead," Rocco finished. "We were checking morgues, but when we turned up nothing, we suspected your body might be in the river. We were running out of options when Bianca arrived. She's the reason we found you."

"It still took you weeks." The rage vanished from his tone, and he stepped back from the desk.

"Things like this do not happen overnight. We had to move cautiously or risk your safety."

"What do you know about my safety?" Paxton glared at Rocco. "I fought to stay alive in there every fucking day. If I wasn't in the hole, then someone was trying to kill me because Marco ordered it."

"I understand your anger but we worked as fast as we could. You were in there as a convicted murderer; it wasn't as if we could get you out on bond. It sounds harsh but you're alive and free, that's what counts now."

Before he could stop himself, Paxton launched off the chair, diving for Rocco. Rage bubbled within him unlike anything he'd dealt with before. It was as though he was possessed. It wasn't like him. Something changed inside of him after months in prison.

Elise's hand tightened around his bicep. "Don't, Paxton, this isn't you."

"This is who I am now." His voice was rough and full of anger; he almost didn't recognize it. "Fuck!" He stepped back, putting distance between him and them. Hurting Rocco was the last thing he wanted. After eight years with Phantom Security, Rocco wasn't just his boss, he was also a friend.

"Rage is understandable, but you need to direct it at the person responsible." Elise leaned against the edge of Rocco's desk. "We're not going to let this go, so we need to put a plan together."

"I've already started working on it." Rocco leaned back in his chair. "Mayor Folger has until five o'clock today to resign. Otherwise we take the information we have to the papers."

"Resign?" Elise turned toward Rocco. "He should face criminal charges."

"It will put Bianca in danger." Paxton placed his hands on the back of the chair and met Rocco's gaze. "As much as I'd like revenge on that pompous asshole, I'd rather he walk free than place Bianca in danger. Keeping her safe is my top priority. Which leaves Marco and his crew."

"Marco was taken care of. His position is gone, and I've made contact with the new Don. I believe we'll come to an arrangement with a little time." Before Rocco could explain, his cell phone rang. "Speaking of those arrangements, I'll need to take this. Hang tight."

Paxton didn't like all the unanswered questions but interrupting Rocco while he talked to the new Don would only make the situation worse. Instead, he waited patiently, something he seemed to acquire more of while he was incarcerated.

"Let's get a coffee. Rocco will need a few minutes." Elise nodded to the far end of the office at the coffee bar and seating area. Without waiting for him to follow, she headed over to the station and began to pull coffee mugs out of the cabinet above. "I understand your anger. After Bianca arrived, I was there, too. It was like being pulled back in time. When Flash was arrested on murder charges, I thought I would lose it. I wanted to go down there and break him out. Those same emotions and overwhelming sense of failure came back."

"You got him out, just like you guys got me out." He took hold of the coffee pot and began to pour it into the mugs. "Look at things with you and Flash now. Happily married."

"You and Bianca seem to have the same spark." She glanced up at him. "I know you went through torment. I read your prison file and the medical report after you were shanked, so I know you went through hell. The question is can you let go of the rage you have for Marco so it doesn't come between you and Bianca?"

"I'd do anything for her." He didn't even need to think about it. "But as long as he's alive, she's in danger. We both are."

"Having him killed could be the dividing wedge between you two. Can you live with that?"

He lifted the mug of coffee and nodded. "As much as the idea kills me, I'd rather lose her and know she was safe than let him live and have her in my arms knowing danger stalks us. With Marco alive, it will only be a matter of time before something happens."

The thought of losing her tightened his chest, making the next breath almost impossible. He loved her so completely he'd sacrifice himself to save her. She was the bright spot in his life, making everything else worth it. He fell in love with her the moment their eyes met and over time that love had only grown stronger.

Unable to sit around the condo any longer, Bianca needed some fresh air. She wasn't sure the danger was completely gone, but if she sat there even for another moment, she'd go insane. Stir crazy, she grabbed her wallet and pulled out a few bucks to buy lattes at the coffee shop on the first floor of the building. She'd go down there, get the lattes and something sweet they could share after Paxton's meeting with Rocco. That's all she needed, a little break.

Before she could allow her fear to get the best of her, she grabbed Paxton's keys and headed for the door. As she made her way to the elevator, she reassured herself everything would be fine. A breath of fresh air and a walk to stretch her legs. After being cooped up for so long, she needed this. While she was staying at Rocco's penthouse, the contract guards left no way for her to sneak off. Even once they went to Chicago there had been guards watching her every move. Now Paxton was back, she could get on with her life. Marco was in jail and while that didn't mean he wouldn't try to cause issues, it was going to make things difficult. Her next challenge was going to be finding a way to get in touch with him.

Somehow, she'd make him see she loved Paxton and that hurting him would hurt her. They were siblings, surely the words he said in anger he couldn't have meant. Even though they were only connected through their father, he was the last family she had. It might take a miracle, but she had to make him see things in a different way.

How different would her life have been if she had been a boy? Or if she had been born to Marco's mother and raised with them? Would she have known about their criminal lifestyle all her life? Would she have been forced to join them? All the questions circled through her mind as she strolled into the coffee shop.

"A high ranking Mexican Cartel member was killed near the U.S. border. More to come after this break."

The news reporter's statement stopped her in her tracks. Even if she could get her brother to see things differently, other issues would continue to haunt them. Would they ever be able to move past the baggage she brought? With Marco in jail, would the cartel or their hired gun, Pieces, come after her instead? Screwing over the cartel was insane. She couldn't figure out what Marco had been thinking. Father left them both with enough money to ensure they'd be set for life. Surely, he didn't have to do what he did. Had one of Marco's crew betrayed him and that's how he found himself in the situation? It almost seemed easier to blame it on a crew member rather than place the blame where it belonged—on Marco.

The hair on the back of her neck stood up, and she glanced around the café. Something was off; she could feel it in every cell of her body. Forgetting the coffee, she spun around and headed toward the elevator. There, across the lobby, she spotted the threat.

Even surrounded by other people coming and going, Gino stood out. His dark black hair combed back as he tried to hide its slight curl. The dark sunglasses hid his eyes, but she could feel his gaze on her.

Without taking her gaze off him, she continued toward the elevator. Five feet, that's all she had to go until she was safely on her way to another floor. She'd alert Paxton or Rocco, and they'd send security. No, Paxton would try to handle it himself, and the very thought of that chilled her blood.

She stopped in her tracks, debating if she wanted to confront Gino herself. Without taking her gaze completely off him, she scanned the area in search of the security Rocco mentioned but found nothing. If she could draw their attention, they might be able to help, and she could keep Paxton out of it. No security guards and she couldn't even spot a security camera. *What kind of building is this without security guards or cameras?*

There was no doubt he was there for her, but if she could keep Paxton safe, she'd sacrifice herself. He had already been through so much with Marco sending him to prison; she didn't want him to suffer anything else because of her. She took a step forward, and Gino's eyebrow rose. His lips parted clearly, surprised by her courage.

A figure stepped in front of her, blocking her view of Gino. "Ms. DeMeo I have orders to escort you to Mr. Arquette's office. If you'll please come with me."

"I ahh…" She glanced up at the man and recognized him as one of Rocco's security guards.

"Ms. DeMeo, it's important you follow me." The security guard urged.

Glancing behind the guard, she realized Gino was gone. With the opportunity to confront him lost, she wasn't sure what else to do, leaving her only one option. She nodded. "Let's go."

I won't allow you to get yourself killed for me. I love you too much for that, Paxton. I'll find a way to get us both out of this.

Chapter Eleven

Paxton stared at the envelope on Rocco's desk, dropped off by a courier only moments before, changing everything. The contents sent Paxton's rage rising until it seeped from every pore as he paced in Rocco's office. He wanted revenge, but before he could extract it, the opportunity had been stripped from him. No words could express the fury coursing through his veins. That bastard, Marco, had more coming to him than Paxton planned to deliver, but he wanted to be the one to end his life. Bianca might not understand, but it was the only way to keep her safe. She could be mad with him all she wanted, but if it came down to her wrath or her death, he'd deal with her anger any day of the week.

"You need to take a second and think about this. He's dead, that's what matters." Rocco sat behind his antique desk calm as if the news didn't change anything.

"He's dead, but Bianca's in more danger." He threw the crumpled letter back at Rocco. "That fucker wants her. It's not about blood now, it's about...." He closed his eyes and could see the letter as if he was still holding it. *Marco paid me to kill the old man, promising me the girl for my trouble. He double crossed me, and now, they're both dead. You have twelve hours to turn the girl over, or you'll join them.*

"We'll deal with it." Elise leaned against the edge of Rocco's desk, her gaze on him. "We're not going to let anything happen to her."

"How are you going to protect her from the mafia?" He screamed. The message had been from Gino, but how many people did he have in his pocket? He was one of Marco's top men; he had a whole crew following his lead.

"Let's calm down, and talk about this." Rocco's voice was even, with only a hint of anger.

"Talk about this? Are you out of your mind?" He slammed his hand down on the edge of Rocco's desk. "There's nothing to talk about. It's time for action. I've got to get her out of here."

"Don't be rash. She's safer here than anywhere else," Elise reasoned.

"She's safe here." Rocco nodded, leaning back in his chair. "But I've got another plan."

"Plan?" Knowing Rocco, Paxton realized he most likely wouldn't like this plan. "We're not using her as bait."

"Not bait per se." Rocco brought an image up on the screen. "I purchased this a few months ago."

"The old hospital?" Elise shook her head. "I don't like where this is going."

"Me either." Paxton took in the image on the screen and had to admit it did provide some advantages they didn't have here. "I'm sure I'm not going to like this, but what are you thinking?"

"As you might expect, the first piece of business was to get the top floor converted into the penthouse suite."

"Obviously." Elise chuckled. "Only to you, Rocco, only you."

"If I'm going to travel back and forth to check on the progress I want to have somewhere comfortable to stay." Rocco didn't even glance at his sister-in-law. "It's a good thing they finished last week because we need it now. Tanner and Brady are already there with a team. We've got the place covered, and if anyone comes around, it will appear as though they're part of the work crew. The grounds and building already have security cameras installed, so Elise and Flash will monitor them from here."

"Moving her will put her in danger."

"Staying here will put her in more danger. He knows where she is." Flash strolled toward them and held out an e-tablet to him. "They were less than fifty feet apart moments ago. If Chet hadn't found her in time, we would have already been too late to save her."

"Where is she?" Paxton demanded. His gaze scanned over the tablet and the images displayed only made his blood boil.

"Chet has her; they're on their way up now."

He didn't care about Rocco's plans. At the moment, he could only focus on one thing: getting to Bianca. He stepped around Flash and jogged out of the office toward the elevators.

"He's bringing her here." Flash called after him, but it didn't slow him down. He needed to see for himself that she was okay.

Why did she leave his condo? Was she leaving him? The notion he might have lost her even if Gino wasn't a factor had him clenching his fist. Angry at himself more than anything, he was on the verge of letting his temper overpower him. Until Bianca came into his life, he hadn't thought much about love. It gave a person a weakness, and in his profession, a weakness could get them killed. Now he had her, he wasn't about to give her up without a fight. He finally understood what love was. He witnessed it with Flash and Elise but she had been an FBI agent before coming to Phantom Security. She was used to field work and the danger it brought with it. Flash had to accept she wasn't going to take herself out of the field just because they were married. Instead, they teamed up to make an unstoppable pair.

As he stepped into the security firm's reception area, Chelsea rose from behind the desk, but he ignored her as the elevator doors opened. He spotted Bianca. Her gaze locked onto his, and for once, he wasn't able to read her expression.

"Paxton…"

"Come with me." As she neared, he turned and headed to his own office. Before he could deal with Rocco and decide what their next move was going to be, he needed a moment with her. He needed to know what she intended to do when she left the safety of his condo.

He opened the door to his office and nodded for her to go ahead before following her inside and shutting the door. Unlike Rocco's office, it wasn't as spacious or as nicely decorated. The solid hardwood L-shaped desk looked empty with only his work laptop and a few pieces of paper scattered on the surface. His black leather office chair was pushed in, serving as a reminder it had been months since anyone sat behind it. The two light blue chairs in front of the desk were the only other furniture.

"You're mad, aren't you?" Standing there in the middle of his office, she looked as if she belonged. Yet all he could think about was stripping her out of the pair of fitted black jeans and gold sweater. He wanted her naked and stretched out on his desk as he slammed his cock into her, riding her hard until she screamed his name in pleasure.

"Why'd you leave?" He tried to keep his voice even, but even to his own ears, he could hear the pain. The idea of losing her now nearly sent him into a blind rage.

"Leave?" She stepped toward him, the soft clink of her heels seemed louder as the moment stretched on. "You think I was leaving you? Oh, baby…" Her hand brushed across his chest before he forced himself to step back.

"Don't play coy." The images he'd seen on Flash's e-tablet proved she considered going to Gino before Chet stepped in. "I saw you…"

"You saw me what? I was going to the café. I needed a little fresh air and coffee. I planned to pick up something sweet we could enjoy when you came

92

back. If you don't believe me here's proof." She reached into the pocket of her jeans and pulled out his keys. "I took your keys with me. I was coming back."

"You put yourself in danger for fucking coffee." He grabbed her wrist, quickly spinning her around so her back pressed against the door. "What were you thinking?"

"I'm sorry…I wasn't." She leaned back, letting her head rest against the door and her gaze drift up to him. "Part of me thought it was over. I had you back, and Marco's in jail. I wanted some semblance of a normal life, but Gino…he's not going to give up. Is he?"

"I'm going to deal with it. Not you, me." His hand caressed the side of her hip. "Do you understand?"

"How is that fair? You can protect me, but I can't protect you. Is that how this works?"

"This is my job." Her body stilled under his touch.

"Your job?" Rage burned in her hazel eyes, turning them a shade darker. "That's what this is…a job? How could I forget that's how this started? I was nothing more than a job to you. At least, now, the truth comes out." She tried to pull away from him, but he was like a brick wall, keeping her in place.

"That's not what I meant." As she tried to pull her wrist from his grasp, he tightened his grip. "Listen to me, darling."

"Screw you!"

"You're so fucking sexy when you're angry." He raised his hand from her hip, tangled it in her hair, and leaned down, pressing their foreheads together. "Not a job as in work, but job as in you're my woman, it's my duty to protect you. Fuck, Bianca, I love you. I want you by my side every day and in my bed every night. I want you as my wife."

"Your wife?" Her voice was whisper soft.

A knock on the door startled her, and she grabbed onto him.

"Yes?" Not sure who was on the other side of the door, but for them to get that far into the Phantom Security, he knew it was an employee and not a threat. Yet he brought her closer to him, his gun hand ready if he needed his weapon.

"Mr. Arquette is waiting," Chet announced from the other side of the door.

"Give me a minute." He pressed his lips to her forehead. "I was serious about what I said. I'm going to make sure you're safe because I want you in my life, always."

"Paxton." She grabbed hold of his shirt, stopping him from pulling away. "The thought of leaving you never crossed my mind. Being with you is the only place I want to be."

"Good, then stay here while I finish with Rocco. When I come back, we'll get out of here and get you somewhere safe."

"I'm safe as long as I'm with you." She let go of his shirt and stepped away from the door. "And Paxton."

"Yes?"

"I'd be honored to be Mrs. Paxton Payne." She shot him a bright smile as he opened the door.

"Chet, I need you to stay with her. If Rocco gave you other orders, I'll deal with him. Do not let her out of your sight until I get back. Understand?" With a nod from Chet, he glanced back at Bianca. "Do you understand?"

"I'm not going anywhere." As if to prove her point, she sank down into one of the plush light blue chairs in front of his desk.

Feeling more comfortable, he headed down the hall toward Rocco's office. Rocco was right; they needed to get her out of there. Gino knew where she was, making it only a matter of time until he made his move. They put everyone at risk by keeping her there.

"We've got enough man power here to keep her safe. Allowing Paxton to take her and run, we lose our advantage. You're putting them both at risk."

Elise argued, her back to the door as Paxton entered.

"His actions are keeping her safe, keeping everyone safe. Gino knows where she is, putting everyone in danger. Getting her out of here will give us a new advantage." Paxton strolled toward them. Gino knowing her location was more than enough reason to get her out of there. She had been in danger before, but now, it was too close to home. He couldn't lose her, not after he just got her back. She was his everything, and he'd die to protect her.

"Gino's not stupid enough to breach the building. He has no idea what floor she's on. We've alerted security, and we're handling it." Elise tried again. "Give us a chance to handle this. They could stay in the penthouse. No one can get up there without a security card, and the helicopter is on the roof if you need a quick escape."

Flash placed his hand on her shoulder. "El, I agree with Rocco and Paxton on this one. She's in too much danger here. We know Gino's already been in the lobby and on the eighth floor; it's only a matter of time before he makes it further. We can't risk everyone's safety. You might not like what I'm about to say, but I won't stand for you being in danger in our home. You mean too much to me."

"There are too many risks to keep her here. Not just to her but to everyone in the building." Not willing to discuss it any longer, Paxton turned his attention to Rocco. "This hospital you're having converted. How close is it to civilians? How many people are we putting at risk if I take her there?"

"It's on more than a hundred acres. That's the reason I've purchased it. There's also a second building which in the past housed staff. Eventually it will be used as a new recruit training center. We're growing, and it's time we add to our manpower. There's no way we're going to be able to keep up with the jobs otherwise," Rocco explained. "Virginia is the perfect place to do that, and by the end of the year, I'll have it functioning."

"You're leaving New York?" Elise raised an eyebrow at him. "You never said."

"Not leaving completely, more like dividing my time. I still love the city and have numerous contacts I'll need to meet with here. Virginia puts us closer to Washington D.C. Many of our jobs come from there and being closer has its benefits," he explained before turning his attention back to Paxton. "Hawk will be there in twenty."

Paxton nodded. Hawk was the best sharpshooter on the team, followed by Grim. Having either of them there would improve their odds dramatically. "We'll get a bag packed and be ready in twenty. Am I taking my own car?"

"Helicopter," Flash informed. "Your vehicle might be compromised. We're not sure, and while we have a team headed there now, we don't have time to wait for results. We'll get you both out of here and deal with what we need to."

"Don't worry, if Gino doesn't follow, we'll deal with him." Rocco grinned. "It will be an honor to get my hands on that bastard."

"It would seem Gino has been in a restricted area. You know how Rocco is when it comes to that," Elise explained.

"Someone's going to have hell to pay." He didn't have an ounce of pity for whoever screwed up. Their neglect put Bianca and everyone else in danger. This was the reason Rocco had such strict security measures. With their business, the risks were too great. They had to keep the other tenants of the building safe.

"Get your woman, and let's put this plan in action," Rocco ordered.

"One request, don't close me out of this. If I'm going to protect her, I need whatever information you have. No matter what it is. If you know anything, I have the right to know. I can't protect her if you don't let me know what challenges we're facing, and she can't stay locked away for the rest of her life. I need to get back to my work for Phantom Security, and she needs to get on with her life, so we can begin our new life together."

"You have my word no one is closing you out. You're part of this team, and Bianca has proven herself to be an asset, too," Rocco reassured him. "Have you told her Marco is dead?"

"Fuck." In the mist of the danger to her, Marco hadn't crossed his mind. "I'll deal with it when we get there. I need to get her out of here first."

"The longer you wait, the harder it's going to be." Rocco warned before glancing at his computer again.

"You pack, and I'll get you all the information you need for the location. It will be on your tablet before you take off." Elise grabbed her laptop from the side of Rocco's desk and headed back to her office.

"Jac and Grim are flying out with you. They'll meet you on the rooftop in twenty," Flash added before following his wife.

"Paxton," Rocco called before he could leave. "Bianca's come to mean a lot to all of us here. Keep her safe."

"Don't worry, I will. Thank you." Without waiting for Rocco to reply, he headed out and down toward his office. Time was short, leaving him rushed to fill her in on the plan and pack before heading to the helicopter. This was about to end one way or another, either here in New York or in Virginia. Gino signed his own death certificate when he came after Bianca. *Fuck with my woman, and I'll fuck up your world.*

Chapter Twelve

Standing in the middle of Rocco's new penthouse condo in Virginia should have put Bianca at ease. She was more than four hours away from where she last spotted Gino. Even if he learned where they were heading, he was still hours behind them. Elise had learned moments before the helicopter left that Gino had a warrant out for his arrest. She hadn't explained why, but she could put her own conclusions together. No matter the reason, it meant flying was out of the question. He'd have to make the drive.

"Are you okay?" Paxton came up behind her and wrapped his arms around her waist.

"I'm as good as can be expected." She leaned back into him, pressing her head against his chest. "I can't believe Marco is dead."

"I'm sorry, darling." He pressed his lips to her temple.

"I should feel something more, but I don't. I'm numb." She slid her hand over his. "He's my brother, but it's as though you told me a stranger died. I'd grieve more for a stray dog than I am for my own brother."

"Look at all he's done. Surely, anyone would have trouble dealing with that." He squeezed her tighter to him. "Right now, you're angry, but you'll grieve for the man you knew and the connection you might have had if things were different. Don't expect to grieve the same as when you lost your father. It will be different if only for the fact you were not as close to Marco as your father."

"He killed my parents." Her voice was barely above a whisper.

"I know." He gently turned her around to face him.

"He put you in prison." She looked up at him. Their gazes locked, and he shook his head. "It's stupid to say it all aloud when you already know all of this, but it makes me feel better saying it. Maybe then I'm not evil for being relieved he's dead."

"Darling, you're not evil. Marco was, and if you knew half the shit he's done since taking over for your father, you would know his death makes the world a little safer. More important, you'll be safer with him dead."

"Not until Gino's dead." She stepped back out of his embrace. "What if someone else comes after me next? The longer I'm around you, the more danger you're in."

"I'm going to take care of this, and you're not going anywhere. I told you, it's my job to protect you. I'm going to make sure you're safe."

"At what cost?" She strolled over to the kitchen bar and placed her hand onto of the granite counter before grabbing the pad laying there. Without glancing down at the hand-drawn map with the little x's marking the positions of each member of the team, she held it up to him. "How many people are at risk because of me?"

"This is what we do," he reasoned.

"I'm not a job, I'm your…" She stumbled over the next part because she wasn't sure what she was to him. Girlfriend? It seemed more than that, especially after their conversation back in his office. Yet fiancée wasn't right either. "I don't want people putting their lives on the line because of me."

"It's all going to be over soon, you need to bear with it a little bit longer." He strolled toward her. "I'm going to finish this, and then we're going to make it official."

"What?"

"Fiancée…no." He looped his arm around her waist and pulled her against the front of him. "I don't think I can wait. I want you as my wife as soon as possible."

"Find a priest." The idea of being his wife suppressed all the doubt of everything else. She gave into the moment and let her worries slip away to allow herself to enjoy the moment. "Go on, I know you want to check things out. I spotted a large hot tub in the master bath so I think I'll take a bath."

"I'll be back before you can miss me." He pressed his lips to hers in a quick kiss. "Then I'm going to make you forget all your worries."

"I'm looking forward to it." She stood there watching as he made his way toward the door. The way his butt filled out his jeans made her fingers ache to touch him. *Damn that man lights fires within me I didn't know existed.*

With the layout of the building fresh in his mind, Paxton strolled into the bedroom. He hoped to find Bianca still soaking in the bathtub, but there she sat on the edge of the bed, a towel wrapped around her body. Her long, brown hair hung down around her shoulders, hiding her face from view.

He stood in the doorway, his gaze glued to her. Every time he looked at her, he was taken by her beauty, but in moments like this when he could watch her without her knowing, there was something more to her. The fire burning within her seemed to dull and instead of the unstoppable woman she tried to be, he could see another side of her. Those moments were when her true beauty shined through. There was no front hiding her emotions, or the strong shell she wore to keep her safe. The emotions she tried to keep hidden from everyone could be seen, and without the veil keeping her hidden, the real side of her emerged. This was the Bianca he had fallen in love with.

"Gorgeous." His voice was barely above a whisper, but it was enough for her to jerk her head up and look at him.

"I didn't hear you come in." She leaned over and continued to rub lotion on her legs. "After you left, I checked. Rocco had the place stocked. If you give me a few minutes to get dressed, I'll make dinner."

"I've already decided what I'm having." In one quick move, he tugged his dark blue polo shirt out of his jeans and over his head.

"Huh?" Without looking at him, she reached over and placed the lotion bottle on the nightstand.

"You, darling." He unhooked his belt, pulling his gun holster from it before placing it on the edge of the ebony nightstand so it would be within reach, and stepped out of his jeans and boxers.

"I know men think with their dicks, but you have other needs besides sex." She shook her head. "You know like sleep and food."

"Don't worry, darling. I'll make sure you're fed, and we can sleep later." He grabbed hold of the edge of her towel, untwisting it so it would come open. "We've got a lot of time to make up for."

"I'm not complaining." She reached out and put her hand on the curve of his hip as she glanced up at him. "You let me sleep while you met with Rocco earlier. As for food, I could care less about it. I'd rather be in bed with you."

"Lie back against the pillows and spread your legs." Without hesitation, she did as he asked, creating a strong contrast with her tanned skin and the white comforter. He joined her on the bed, kneeling between her arched legs. He slipped his fingers between her legs, sliding his thumb over her clit. He thrust his fingers into her as his thumb continued to pull more pleasure from her until she was wiggling against his touch. "So fucking beautiful."

"Paxton…" She tried to reach out to him, but he leaned back, moving out of her reach.

"I love how your body reacts to me." Sliding a finger into her, he leaned down and kissed her inner thigh. "The way you arch into my caresses and the fire burning in your eyes. Do you have any idea what you do to me?"

Arching up slightly, she nodded to his hard cock. "The proof is hard to deny."

"Not just physically." He nipped her thigh, making her jerk against his hand as he continued to pump in and out of her. "With my profession, I didn't believe love had a spot in my life. You showed me I need more in my life than just my career. If having you in my life means leaving Phantom Security, I'm okay with it. I can do anything as long as I have you by my side. I love you, Bianca."

"Come here." She wrapped her hand around his wrist, doing her best to pull it away from her pussy. "Please, Paxton."

He slipped his finger out of her and rose to arch over her, angling himself so his cock was brushing against her pussy, keeping her on edge. "Yes?"

"Damn you, stop that."

"What?" His lips curled into a smile as he pumped his hips, teasing himself along her.

"You make it hard to think straight." Her hands grabbed hold of his hips, doing what she could to keep him still. "I wanted to say you'd never have to quit. Your job brought us together, and I won't allow it to divide us. Just don't lie to me again. Whatever happens, we can overcome it."

"You have my word. Now, can I get back to what I was doing?" He dipped his head to the crook of her shoulder.

"Get back to it…you mean like this?" She reached between them, wrapping her hand around the base of his cock, before slowly sliding her hand down as far as she could. "I can't get enough of you. I need you, Paxton." Her nails dragged along his cock, adding to the pleasure.

"I know I'll never get enough of your naked body." Breaking her hold on him, he rolled over, taking her with him, making her squeal. With her on top, he slid his hands over her hips.

"You're going to leave me in control." Her eyes widened. "I could get used to this."

"Just as I could get used to you riding me, with your breasts bouncing. Now get to work, darling, before I change my mind."

She arched over his cock, and he shifted his hips slightly, adjusting his angle. He slid his cock along her folds, teasing her until she sucked in her bottom lip and bit it, a moan escaping her throat. Unable to take it any longer, he grabbed hold of her hips, pushing her down as he arched his hips upward, sliding his dick into her until he buried himself to the hilt. He kept his hands on her hips, helping her work his shaft up and down. With each pump, she began to gain more control, needing him less. As she began to set her own pace, he moved his hands away from her hips and let them roam over her body.

Watching her above him, her tits bouncing with every move she made, he wasn't sure how long he could hold back. Instead of focusing on his own desire, he reached up to fondle her breasts, sliding his fingers over the hard buds of her nipples, teasing them. With his touch, her pace increased, making each thrust faster as she drove herself up and down and his need to give into his release increased.

"Oh, Paxton!" She tipped her head back, growing closer to ecstasy.

He grabbed hold of her hips and drove his cock into her harder and faster. As much as he wanted to make it last, he needed this release as much as she did. The frenzy had her moaning until she called out his name, groaning as her climax sent her over the edge. The walls of her pussy clenched around him, breaking his control and moments later, he buried himself deep within her one final time.

She collapsed forward, burying her head near his collarbone. Reaching up, he pushed her hair to the side and kissed along her neck, working his way to her ear. "You're fucking amazing."

"You're not half bad yourself." She mumbled, her breath coming in hot pants against his skin. "Forget dinner, I'm going to stay right here."

As if agreeing his cock twitched, hardening against the walls of her pussy. "I've always been a fan of a double feature." Before he could put his plan into motion, his earpiece crackled to life.

Paxton, I'm about two miles up the road, and there's a car here. It's a rental with a New York license plate.

"Shit." He grabbed hold of her hips, and in one quick movement, he lifted her off him. "Sorry, darling."

"What's going on?" She sat up and grabbed the towel, quickly pulling it back over her body. "What changed?"

Tugging on his jeans, he kept his eyes on her, watching as the shields she kept up slammed back into place. He needed to do something about that, but it would have to wait until later. First, they had a bigger issue. He reached up, flicking the device on allowing his team to hear him. "I'm on my way down. Brady, see if you can find anything the driver might have left behind, then backtrack and find him."

"Paxton?" He held his hand up, stopping her.

"Tanner, get Hawk and Grim in place. I don't want any surprises." He ordered before ending communication on his end. "Bianca, I need you to get dressed and stay here. I'll be back as soon as I check the security feeds. This would be easier if the command center in Rocco's office was functional."

"He's here, isn't he? Gino found us."

"He's not going to get this far. Trust me. We've got the grounds covered. Hawk and Grim are the best there is." He grabbed hold of her wrist and pulled her up from the bed. "I'm going to protect you."

"Promise you'll come back to me." Her voice trembled as she clearly fought for control over her emotions.

"I promise." He pressed his lips to hers in a quick kiss. "I'll be back before you have a chance to miss me."

"I already miss you."

Torn between wanting to keep her at his side where he could protect her and wanting her to stay in the condo where she'd be safe, he forced himself to grab his gun from the bedside table and walk out of the bedroom. She was safer there than she was a few floors below. If Gino showed up, he didn't want his attention diverted from taking down the man that was ultimately her biggest threat. *I'm going to end this here and now.*

Chapter Thirteen

Standing in the security room, Paxton couldn't shake the knot in his stomach. Something was off. His instincts kept him alive all his life. First, as a police officer in New York's gang squad, then on jobs with Phantom Security, and lastly in prison. He knew enough not to ignore them. He couldn't determine what the problem was. Even Tanner seemed more on edge.

"Something's wrong." Tanner's gaze shifted over the monitors. "If he's here, we should have located him by now."

"A rental car from New York parked two miles away is too much of a coincidence to overlook. He has to be here." Paxton rolled his shoulders, trying to ease the tension building within them. "I don't like this."

"Why don't you go upstairs?" Tanner brought his coffee mug to his lips and took a sip. "I'll let you know if we find anything. Hawk and Grim are in position. Brady has a team out with him searching the area. We'll find him if he's here."

Before he could take Tanner's suggestion, Paxton's phone rang. *Elise.* He hit the answer button and brought it to his ear. "What did you find?"

"The car was stolen," Elise answered.

"There's no security footage of him or the car leaving the city." Flash added, making it clear he was on speaker phone. "We're checking security cameras between us and you, but without knowing what route he took, it's going to take some time."

"Can you confirm he's gone?" He didn't know why he asked. The evidence was piling up to prove it already.

"No concrete proof, but you know as well as I do he's not here. I don't know how we missed him." Flash bitched. "You guys need to be ready."

"We'll send more manpower." Rocco's voice came through the phone, making Paxton wonder if anyone else was there.

"I think we've got it covered. We've got the best of the team here, well besides the three of you." His lips curled into a smile. He'd worked with Rocco enough times to know even though he was the man behind the company, he was also one Paxton would trust at his back on any mission. He was one of the best. Since Flash and Elise joined the company, they'd proven themselves, too. They weren't just management; they were part of the team. Phantom Security wouldn't be the same without them.

"Fine, keep us updated." Flash added before the line went dead.

Paxton slipped his phone back into his pocket and turned his attention back to Tanner. "That confirms it. Gino's here. Now we need to find him."

"I've got everyone we can spare out there searching. Hawk and Grim are watching from above, and I'm monitoring the security cameras. There's not much we can do until he makes his presence known. You should be with her. Let us handle this."

"Alert me if you find anything." He glanced at the screen and noticed something different. "That door…"

"What?" Tanner leaned closer to the screen Paxton's gaze was locked on.

"Rewind the footage." Paxton focus stayed on the screen as Tanner did what he was asked. One second the door was completely closed, the next it was slightly ajar. Something changed. "Again."

As the footage replayed Paxton wasn't focused on the door any longer, rather his attention was on the timestamp. "Fuck!"

"That's not possible." Tanner shook his head. "How did he get into the building?"

"The better question is how did he bypass our security?" Paxton glanced at the camera number, quickly locating the position on the map and headed for the door. "Get the team back here, and get Hawk to the penthouse. Watching the grounds is useless now he's already in the building. I want Bianca safe. I'm going after Gino. Have the team meet me there when they get back."

"I want to know if you see anything on the monitors." Tanner grabbed two bulletproof vests and tossed one at Paxton. "Let's do this."

"I need you here."

"You're not going alone. Sid can handle watching the monitors." Falling into step with Paxton, Tanner ordered the team to their new location and Hawk to the penthouse.

Rather than taking time to argue, Paxton headed down the two flights of stairs to where the door had suddenly opened. He didn't know if Gino was still there, or where he might have gone after he passed through the door. With him bypassing the security system, it meant he could be anywhere. Part of him wanted to head to the penthouse. That would be Gino's end game, and being there, meant he could protect Bianca. First, he'd check this out, and if nothing came of it, he'd go upstairs. The team could flush him out and up. Upstairs he'd wait, with Bianca safe further in the penthouse, away from Gino's grasps or stray bullets.

"It's empty." Hawk's voice echoed through the earpiece.

"Fuck!" Paxton growled.

"Keep a level head man, Bianca needs you." Tanner pulled his gun from his holster, ready for whatever they encountered.

That was easier said than done. He witnessed first-hand what Gino did to his victims. The horrors he put them through before leaving their bodies an unidentifiable mass flashed before his eyes. The thought of Bianca being at his mercy was enough to send him over the edge. It was time to end this. *I'm coming for you Bianca.*

Groggy and disoriented Bianca forced herself to open her eyes. For a moment, she expected to wake up in bed, but the moment she opened her eyes and found herself staring at an old hospital room, she knew she wasn't in the penthouse. She moved her hand, reaching out for anything she could use for a weapon, but instead of being able to move she found herself strapped down to a gurney. Her head hurt and she could taste blood. Instantly, she remembered Gino's hand around her neck as she struggled to breathe. Gino's words echoed through her thoughts again. *Keep fighting and you'll never see your boyfriend alive again. I've already got him tied up downstairs.* Her world went dark, and the only image in her mind was Paxton. If she died, he'd blame himself. It wasn't his fault; it was hers.

"I wondered how long it would take you to come around." Gino stood above her with a knife in hand. "Now, we can have some fun. What do you think I should send your lover? How about a finger?" The blade teased along her ring finger. "An ear." Quickly shifting positions, he brought the blade up to her ear, pressing the sharp point against her skin until she bled.

"Where is he?"

"Always so naïve." He teased the blade down her shoulder blade, leaving behind a red cut. Thin but deep enough it bled. "I could ask you why you think if I caught him I would keep him alive, but then I did just ask you what body part you wanted to send to your lover, so that implies he's alive."

"You never had him. You lied to me." She cursed herself for falling for his play on words. Paxton would never trade her life for his. He'd have never told Gino how to get into the condo, even if he was offered a deal to spare his life. Paxton was more of a man than Gino would ever be; he'd rather die than turn her over to him. *I'm sorry Paxton...so sorry. I should have believed you.*

"Your man left you here to die, but I want him to know what I did to you before I killed you."

Her heart raced in her chest, but she refused to look away from him. "Please, Gino, it doesn't have to be like this. We can go away together. Anywhere you want."

"Stupid bitch! Trying to save your lover won't work." Gino spat, shoving the blade into her forearm and slicing a long, deep gash.

"Ahh!" She screamed as blood trickled down to pool under her arm.

"That asshole came into the family and tried to destroy us. Now I'm going to be the one to destroy him. I've already rigged a bomb. I'm going to blow this building up, destroying him and those closest to him. Nothing personal against you, but he's had this coming since he stepped foot in Chicago. I tried to tell Marco, but he wouldn't listen. I knew something was up with him. When I found out he was fucking you, I went to Marco, knowing he'd take care of him. Then I thought he'd finally give you to me like we agreed, but he said he had bigger plans for you." He leaned in closer, so his face was above hers. "Your brother broke his word. Do you know what happens to liars?"

"Gino—"

"We cut out his tongue, so he can't continue his lies." He gripped her arms, digging his fingers into her as the blade sliced into her flesh again. "For Marco, I ensured he'll spread no more lies. The dead speak no more."

A single tear rolled down her cheek. She already knew her brother was dead, but Gino's words stabbed to her heart. It reminded her once again she never got the chance to make Marco see Paxton was a good man. More than that, he was the last family she had left. Images of Marco's mother flashed in her mind. While they despised each other, she couldn't help the twinge of sadness knowing the woman had lost her husband and now her son.

111

"You'd grieve for the bastard who sold you like a whore?" Shaking his head, he stepped away from her and grabbed a vase from the bedside table. The dried flowers still in the vase made her wonder about whoever was in the room before her. Had they died like she was about to? That would explain why the flowers were left behind. If they survived, perhaps she could too. Before hope had time to blossom within her, he threw the vase against the wall. Dried flower petals and shards of glass flew toward her. If her hands were free, she'd have covered her face, but all she could do was turn to the side, doing her best to protect herself. "You're as stupid as he believed you were."

"He was family."

"You know nothing of family." He snapped, pushing the bedside table so it toppled over, sending the abandoned content clattering to the floor.

"Then help me understand, tell me what family means to you." To move past the pain and fear, she tried to focus on what she learned in college and try to get inside his mind. If she stayed strong and focused, someone would find her. Paxton would come back to the condo and find her gone. They'd check the security cameras. She might not see any of Rocco's new high-tech security cameras he installed, but it was there. *Focus.*

"Whores don't understand."

"Let me try. Talk to me, Gino. I can understand if you give me a chance." She paused hoping he'd say something, but he didn't. "To me, family are the ones you spend holidays with. Everyone gathered around a big table, enjoying a delicious meal, talking, and having a good time. It doesn't matter if they're blood related or not. Family can be whoever you want it to be. It's all about the bond you have with them."

"Do you know the memory I cherish most?" As he continued to remain silent, she began to lose hope. "I was at my father's place when you and Marco came back. I don't know where you were, but Marco brought pizza home with him. The four of us sat down together and ate. I remember you giving me the last slice of mushroom and pepperoni because I didn't like the one with sausage and peppers. You hate green peppers, but you did it for me."

"Your father expected it."

"You can use that excuse if you'd like, but there's more to it. You did it for me. I've always remembered that. It was the sweetest thing anyone has ever done for me." Even with her hands tied to the bars on each side of the gurney, she reached out. Her heart pounded viciously against her ribs as she tried not to allow her fear to show. "Come here."

He moved away from the wall, and she forced herself to continue. "That gesture drew my attention to you. It made me want to get to know you better. Then after Father died...I don't know what happened, but you changed."

"It started long before he died." He stood there next to her, not touching but not moving away either. "You had no idea what was happening behind the scenes. Marco was becoming more vindictive, he wanted your father out of the way so he could run things his way."

"Father always kept that side of his life hidden. It wasn't until a couple weeks before he died I learned the truth of his business. Maybe I was naïve. Marco surely dropped enough hints in the months prior. I was too busy with college to really understand or give it any attention. His comments were wrapped in such a way they were easy to miss since I knew nothing of Father's other life. All I knew was he owned an Italian restaurant."

"Marco wasn't having that. He was angry your father allowed you to go to college while he was forced into our lifestyle, yet he wasn't allowed to make his own changes. He wanted to pave his own way, but your father held him back. He had to do everything the way your old man did."

"Is that why he killed my parents?" She tried to remain calm, but the rage and grief seeped back into her.

"He wasn't supposed to be with your mother. He was supposed..." He shook his head and refused to look at her.

"Supposed to what?" Trying not to think about the warm blood pooling under her, she lifted up as much as the ropes binding her to the gurney would allow. The rope running under her breasts to tie somewhere underneath, dug into her ribs, but she fought to get a better look at him. "Don't you think I deserve to know? Wouldn't you want to know if it was your parents? Please, Gino." She hated to beg, but she wanted to know. With Marco dead, who else could she ask? Going back to Chicago would only place her in more danger and that was if she even made it out of there alive.

"He was supposed to be with his wife. Marco wanted his parents' dead…not your mother. Marco adored your mother, he wanted his own to be more like her."

The idea of Marco wanting their father dead had been a blow, knocking her off balance, but the fact he wanted both of his parents' dead took it to a different level. Wanting to take things over could almost explain why he wanted Father out of the way but his mother? What was the reason behind that? Had she not supported his career choice? It didn't make sense because like Bianca had been, she seemed completely ignorant to what was happening around her. She wasn't even sure if she knew what her husband and son had been involved in.

"Why? What did his mother do to make him want her dead?"

"How the fuck would I know?" Gino snapped.

"I'm sorry, I thought…" She relaxed back against the gurney. "Marco's mom didn't seem to care what was happening around her. I can't see her causing problems."

"She doesn't care because she's using the product." He grabbed a baggy she hadn't noticed from the edge of the bed and held it out to her. "Your father who you thought was such a great man got her addicted to the shit to keep her under control. He started with enough to keep her submissive and it backfired big time. Now she's using so much every day it would kill most people. Marco got tired of supporting her addiction. Getting her help would admit there's a problem. The family couldn't have that. They don't want to bring attention to themselves. There'd be too many questions they couldn't answer and draw attention to them."

She eyed the bag of white powder, even though she never saw the stuff before it was clearly cocaine. "Are you using it, too?" She glanced up at him, letting her gaze focus on him.

"This shit isn't for me." He bought the bag closer to her face. "Choice is yours, whore. You choose to leave here with me voluntarily, or I'll make you beg for your next hit. You're going to be mine whether you like it or not. I paid the price for you with blood. Do you understand what I'm saying?"

"There's no need for drugs. I told you I'll do whatever you ask. Come on, Gino, you know me. My word is good. Untie me. There's no reason for this. I'd have come to you if I knew." She focused her gaze on him, trying to show him with her eyes she'd do whatever he wanted.

"I've been hunting you since you ran after your boyfriend was arrested."

"I didn't know it was you." She reached out as far as her bonds would allow, and her finger brushed along the back of his hand. "I didn't know who Marco would send, but I knew he'd want me to pay. Especially after his message."

"He wanted you dead. You betrayed the family when you chose him over us." He reached out and fisted a clump of her hair, pulling, as he leaned forward, his face in front of hers, the stench of alcohol on his breath nearly making her gag. "Do you have any idea what we do to traitors?"

"I didn't know, Gino, you have to believe me. I'd never…" She placed her hand against his side, grabbing hold of his shirt. "I thought he was one of us."

"One of us!" Gino's grip tightened, bringing tears to her eyes. "What do

115

you know about one of us?"

"Please, Gino, you're hurting me." She focused her tear-filled gaze on him. "After Father died, I was brought into things. There are people there I consider friends, family. I wouldn't want anything to happen to you or them."

"You always thought you were better than us. That fancy degree."

"Now, you sound like Marco." The moments the words left her mouth she wished she could take them back. His grip tightened on her hair, and she fought to bring the calmness back to the situation. "I never thought I was better. My college degree means nothing, it's just a piece of paper."

He let go of her hair, and she relaxed back against the gurney. "You showed such disgust every time Marco needed you to do something for the family."

"Because Father wanted me to have nothing to do with it. I was trying to respect his wishes. Those were the last words he said to me. How could I support Marco's wishes when I knew Father was set against it?"

"He was old school. He believed women had no business in this lifestyle." He leaned against the metal frame, allowing her hand to stay on his side. "He's right. Women have a duty to keep house and to bear children for their man. Our lifestyle...it's too dangerous."

"What Marco thought about my degree and me being better than anyone isn't true. I can be the woman you want me to be. Give me a chance." She caressed her hand along his side, teasing her finger under his shirt. Part to show him she was serious, while the other part was looking for his weapon. He was armed. If she could get ahold of it, or at least know where it was, it would give her an advantage she didn't have now. *Please let this work. Hurry, Paxton, I need you.*

Chapter Fourteen

Paxton, followed by Tanner, went through the door Gino had left ajar, instead of it leading to Bianca, the other side only led to another hallway. This section wasn't patched into the new security camera, leaving them blind and making Paxton anxious. The longer Bianca was alone with Gino, the higher the risk was. They needed to find her before he had a chance to hurt her. Paxton pushed open another door, glancing around the room. Nothing. Where the hell were they?

"I found them!" Sid's voice filled his earpiece. "Go straight, third door."

"You sure you've got this?" Tanner glanced at him, as if deciding if he should send Paxton out.

"I'm going for my woman, with or without your support. Either let's do this, or get the fuck out of my way." He moved down the hall. No longer considering anything but getting Bianca back.

"I'm right behind you. Two minutes." Hawk's voice came through the earpiece.

Moving down the hallway, Paxton prepared himself for what they might find behind the door. "Can you see her, Sid?"

"No. Once you're through that door there's a short hallway, fifth door and that's where Gino took her. There's nowhere else for them to go."

"We need to wait for Hawk and the team." Tanner urged before Paxton could open the door.

"Fuck that. It will take them too long to come around."

"Hawk's at the end of the hall. I can see him." Sid explained.

"Give Grim the location, see if he can get into another position in case we need him." Paxton ordered. With the building shaped like a horseshoe, it might be enough to give Grim an angle from another point in the hospital.

"He's scouting locations, now. He'll be in touch if he has a shot," Sid added as his fingers slid over the keyboard sending soft clicks through the earpiece. "I'm searching for another angle to see into the room. Give me a minute before you head in."

Tanner grabbed his arm, stopping him as he opened the door, and Hawk came up behind them. "Let us handle Gino; you worry about getting Bianca."

"I can't get eyes on her. It's been ten minutes since he took her in there…" Sid's voice was strained.

"What?" Hawk demanded.

"She was unconscious when he carried her in. There was blood on her face and shirt."

The urgency in Sid's voice sent Paxton on a rampage. Gino would die before the day was over. Without a moment to spare, he pushed his way passed Tanner and pulled open the door. A loud bang of something crashing to the floor, followed by glass shattering as it hit the floor sped his pace. He kept his gun ready, but not aimed. Tanner and Hawk were on his heels, the three of them moving almost as one as if they had worked together in the past.

"I'd have never run if I knew it was you." Bianca's words stopped him as he neared the door. "Remember what I said about the pizza before?"

"What about it?" Gino replied.

"That night after I left, I thought about you. I wanted to get to know you, maybe go out to dinner. I wanted to make a move to show you I was interested, but Marco…" Something scraped together, sounding almost like metal on metal as Bianca paused. "We don't have to worry about him any longer. Untie me and let's go somewhere new. We can start over together."

"What about your boyfriend?"

"It was over when he lied to me." Subconsciously, he knew what she was doing, she was keeping Gino calm, telling him what he wanted to hear, and buying herself time. Still the words sliced deep into his chest. "He betrayed us."

"Then why did you come to him?"

"What Marco did was wrong. It should have been settled the old fashion way." Bianca grunted and a creak of metal echoed out into the hall. "I wanted my own revenge for what he did. Marco took that away when he sent Anthony to prison."

Anthony. She hadn't called him that since they were reunited. *She's just playing the role. Playing Gino to buy them time to rescue her.*

Let's go. Tanner mouthed as if he realized Paxton was becoming more agitated the longer he listened to her.

Not waiting another second, he stepped into the doorway, his gun raised and quickly focused on Gino. "Step away from her!"

"It's about time you joined the party." Anger had Gino's muscles tight as he glared at him.

"Brady, what's your location?" Sid's voice held a panic that hadn't been there before.

"Just coming onto the floor."

"I need you in the same location, except the fourth door. I repeat fourth door, not the third. There's a bomb!"

Fuck! Paxton wanted to reply to the earpiece conversation, but he didn't want to alert Gino to the fact they uncovered his secondary plan. "I'm the one you're angry with. Now, I'm here. Let her go, and let's settle this. Man to man."

"She's mine." Gino had been untying her as they entered and now stood by the bed. He wasn't touching her, but she was still too close. He glanced behind Paxton and chuckled as he spotted Hawk and Tanner. "It seems you brought company. Three people to rescue your girlfriend. See Bianca, I told you he didn't care about you. I'd have brought a whole army to rescue you if you were my woman."

"That's where we differ. I don't need to bring a fleet of gunpower with me. I'll handle my own dirty work." Paxton kept his gaze focused on Gino, doing his best to keep the other man's attention while Bianca worked on the rest of the ropes binding her to the gurney

"Why don't you let the woman go?" Hawk suggested. "Whatever the issue here is, you two can work it out without her. We start shooting up the place, and she's bound to get caught with a stray bullet. Then you both lose."

"She's mine, she stays with me." Without glancing down at her Gino reached out and wrapped his hand around her arm, digging into the stab wound and making the blood pour out. "Right, whore?"

"Ahh." She moaned in pain. "Please, Gino…my arm."

His other hand moved to his waistband, and Paxton shot. The bullet tore through Gino's shoulder, sending blood splattering on the wall behind him. As he stumbled back, Tanner went to him. Paxton didn't stop him. As much as he wanted Gino dead, he wanted to get Bianca somewhere safe. The bomb in the next room could go off at any moment, ending all their lives. The desire to protect his woman outweighed his need for revenge. She was all that mattered in that moment.

"Paxton!" The moment he stepped close enough, Bianca wrapped her arm around him, pulling him to her. The events crashed down around her, sending her mind into overload. The man she wasn't sure if she'd see again was there in front of her, breaking down her last shred of strength. "I knew you'd

come."

"I'm here, darling. It's going to be okay." Keeping his gun in one hand, he grabbed his knife from his belt and sliced through the remaining ropes. "Can you walk?"

"I'm fine." She nodded as he helped her down from the gurney.

"There's a bomb. We've got to get everyone out." She grabbed hold of his shirt, her gaze locked onto his.

"It's a dud."

"What?" She shook her head.

"Brady just informed me." He tipped his head, and she saw the little black earpiece he was wearing. "We're safe. Now, I want you to go out into the hallway with him and the others. I'll be there in a minute."

Gino slipped out of Tanner's grasp, coming straight for them, before she could process it, Paxton pushed her toward the door. Gino's gun was out and already raised at Paxton. *No!* She wasn't sure if the word had come out aloud or not. Terror froze her in place, and though her mind screamed at her, words would not come.

Paxton dropped the knife and wrapped his other hand around the butt of his gun, bringing it up to focus on Gino. Everything seemed to be happening in slow motion, and she feared he wouldn't be quick enough. Gino was going to shoot him. There was nothing she could do about it.

Gunfire erupted in the room, leaving her standing there unsure what to do as a hand wrapped around her wrist pulling her out of the line of fire.

"No…" Not knowing who it was, she fought against them. It was more than the fact she didn't want to leave Paxton, she wasn't sure if Gino had anyone else with him. She hadn't seen anyone, but it didn't mean others weren't there. Her heart beat furiously in her ears. She couldn't hear anything but the blood pounding and faint pops from the gunshots.

Gino staggered back, blood blossoming from a wound in his chest, tainting his white shirt red. The sight of his blood made her gaze turn to Paxton. She could only see his back and it made her chest tighten. Was he injured? Temptation to go to him gripped her, but fear made her knees go weak, sending her crumbling to the floor. All her training taught her that self-preservation was high for most people, and they'd do whatever they could to get out of danger. Yet her own safety didn't cross her mind.

"She's mine..." Gino's muffled statement was enough to bring her attention back to him.

"I'm not yours! I've never been yours!" She wasn't sure if she spoke loud enough for him to hear her, but to her own ears, it seemed too loud. Speaking the words were freeing. All the lies she told Gino before seemed to disappear from her mind, giving her back her freedom. She hadn't been more than a pawn in his game. Maybe he wanted her because in his sick mind it was a way of getting back at Marco. Now, it was over.

"Min..." Collapsed against the wall, Gino's eyes went lifeless as his life slipped away.

Sitting there on the floor, not even fifteen feet away, she should have felt something. A man died before her eyes, and yet she was numb to it. He killed her parents and her brother. She wasn't sure where her emotions were when it came to her brother, but the idea he was behind the deaths of her whole family was enough to tear old wounds open. She'd grieve for her parents again and for the drama her father's life had brought to her. She'd grieve for her brother, too, but part of her was relieved knowing he would no longer be an issue for her. With Marco and Gino both dead, were her problems over? She wasn't sure, but that was something to handle another day.

"Darling..." A hand brushed across her arm, but she couldn't tear her gaze away from Gino's dead body. "Let's get you out of here."

"Paxton!" She reached for him, only to have the sight of blood stop her. "You're bleeding..."

"It's okay." He wrapped his arm around her and lifted her off the floor. "I'm okay."

She looped her arms around his neck and relaxed into his embrace. "Thank you."

"For what?"

"Coming for me."

"I'd always come for you." He pressed his lips to her forehead. "Let's get you out of here, so Tanner can look at your arm."

She stared up into his eyes, thankful for a man like him in her life. Somehow, she knew with him by her side everything would work out. She wasn't sure how, but she knew it would. For the first time since her father died, she had hope for the future. *For our future.*

Chapter Fifteen

The stress of the long day finally caught up to Bianca as she curled up on the bed. Everything crashed down around her, numbing her from the inside out. Even as Tanner stitched her arm before bandaging it, she didn't feel it. She would later, but at that moment, she was numb. Her family was dead, Gino had tried to kill her, and she had almost lost Paxton. What would she have done then? Everything she wanted in her life seemed to disappear when she thought about the possibility of losing Paxton. She wondered if she was being too needy, clinging to the one solid thing in her life, but even that didn't stop her from wanting what they could have together.

This ordeal had tested her strength, and while she always thought she was strong, she realized she wouldn't have overcome this if it weren't for Paxton, Rocco, and the Phantom Security team. Rocco brought Paxton back to her, and they got her through this. For that, she owed them more than she could ever repay.

I can repay them by leaving and not bringing more danger to them. The thought tightened her chest, and she leaned back against the pillows. Leaving would keep them safe, and she would do it if it weren't for Paxton. After everything she went through to get him back, she didn't want to lose him again. *It's either walk away from him or have him die because of me.*

Even with Marco and Gino dead, she couldn't be sure there wouldn't still be a threat from whoever took over Marco's position. Whoever was in charge now would believe she was a threat. Someone who knew too much information or might want to take back over the family. Reality was she didn't want anything to do with it, and she knew nothing more than a few details Marco had let slip. Even if she had known every detail, it wasn't as if she'd go to the cops. Involving the police would only bring her more trouble, and that was the last thing she wanted. *I just want a peaceful life again. I want to live without worrying about who's lurking in the shadows.*

"You should be sleeping." Paxton strolled through the bedroom door, coming straight for her. His brown hair had grooves from where he continued to drive his hand through it and stress had the lines by his eyes pinched together.

"I was thinking." She adjusted slightly so she could get a better view of him.

"Didn't Tanner give you something for the pain?" He sat on the edge of the bed, but unlike before, he didn't touch her.

"What pain?" No drugs could take away the pain in her heart. Even as he sat close to her, it was clear something had shifted between them, and it was killing her. She couldn't remember a time since their first date they had ever been so close without touching.

"Don't do that, Bianca. Don't try to act like nothing happened. It will only make matters worse."

"Between us?" She shook her head. "Forget I said anything. I'm not in any pain."

"You will be." Unable to meet his gaze, she shifted uncomfortably.

"What happened between us? Things were fine, and now…" She wanted to reach out and touch him, but the idea of him pulling away from her was enough to stop her. A few hours ago, they were making love, and now, he appeared as though he couldn't get away from her fast enough. Had she been a fling while he took care of business, and now that things were done, he was breaking it off with her?

"You need to rest." He stood up but didn't move away from the edge of the bed.

"Paxton." As the conversation with Gino moments before, Paxton had come to her rescue played through her thoughts again she was unable to stop herself from touching him. With her arm, she reached out and took hold of his hand. *It was over when he lied to me...I wanted my own revenge for what he did. Marco took that away when he sent Anthony to prison.* In her mind, she could hear the words she spoke play over and over again. "I didn't mean anything I said to him."

"You think that's what this is about? You think I'm upset because you told him what he needed to hear to protect yourself?" He didn't pull away from her touch, yet he wasn't returning the caress either.

"Then, what is it? There's a change between us, and I don't know what happened. How can I fix something when I don't know what happened to cause it all to go wrong?"

"It can't be fixed." He stepped away from the bed, forcing her to let go of his hand.

"So that's it?" *Don't fight him. Let him walk away, or he'll die because of you.* She tried to remember her earlier thoughts, but her heart didn't care about logic. The love she had for him was too strong to let it end without a fight. There had to be some way for her to have him and keep him safe. That's what she wanted from the beginning; she couldn't give up on it now.

"Look at you, look at what happened to you because of me."

Not feeling any pain, she rose off the bed and went to stand in front of him. "I'm alive because of you. That's what happened."

"Bian—"

"No." She cut him off. "If you're going to end things between us the least you can do is be a man about it. Don't lie to me and blame it on some stupid shit."

"How can you…" He shook his head. "You need to get some rest."

"Screw you!" She went over to the duffle bag with their clothes still inside and grabbed a pair of jeans from the top. "If you can't man up about this, I'm leaving." Leaning over to pull on the jeans, pain blossomed in her stomach, and her knee throbbed. Taking in a sharp breath, she tried to ignore it.

"Fuck, Bianca." He came up behind her, wrapped his arm loosely around her waist, forcing her to stand upright. "You're going to hurt yourself further."

"What do you care? It's over, remember?" Her words sliced through her stomach making her queasy.

"This isn't what I want." With her jeans halfway on, he spun her around to face him. "Look at what happened to you. This is my fault."

"How do you figure that?" She stared into his gaze. "Unless I'm mistaken, Gino's the one responsible. Not you."

"I left you alone. I brought you here."

"You did what you had to in order to keep everyone safe. No one can blame you for that." She pressed her hand against his cheek. "You rescued me."

"He should have never gotten his hands on you."

"He came down the rooftop stairs. How were you supposed to stop him? I heard something, and at first, I thought it was you until he appeared. I tried to get to the elevator, but he was on me before…" She shook her head. "It doesn't matter, it's over."

"That's just it. We don't know if it's over." His eyes closed, but he didn't move away. "By going undercover, I started this whole situation. I'm the reason you're in danger."

"Bullshit." Her stomach churned. "Marco traded me as payment for killing my parents. After Gino completed the task, Marco refused to hand me over. That's why Gino came after me now. It had nothing to do with you."

"Darling, you're not considering the whole picture. If I hadn't interfered with the organization, Marco would still be alive, and you'd still be under his protection. Gino was stupid but not enough to go up against your brother."

"And I'd have spent the rest of my life miserable, eventually in Gino's hands, and Heaven help me then."

He wrapped his arms around her, pulling her against his chest. "You know what he likes to do, don't you?"

"You mean his collection of knives? Or do you mean the torture he puts people through breaking their spirit before eventually killing them? I know all about Gino's dark side. Marco made sure of it. I can't tell you how many times Marco told me if I didn't do what he ordered he was going to let Gino have his fun with me."

"He's dead, now."

"But it's not over, is it?" Knowing the answer without him even speaking, she leaned her head against his chest. She wanted him to hold her like he had before, to allow the love he had for her to wrap around her, but now it was as if there was a brick wall between them. "It's never going to be over."

"Rocco has connections…I'll make the arrangements, and it'll be over for you." He pulled his arms back so he was no longer touching her. Only her head remained on his chest, keeping him from moving away.

"Arrangements? Over for me? What about for you? What are you talking about, Paxton?"

"Think of it as witness protection. A new place, new identity. You'll be safe."

She didn't need a mirror to know her eyes had gone wide with shock as she lifted her head up to look at him. "You can't be serious! After everything we've gone through."

"That's the point." He moved away from her and headed toward the door. "I'll make the preparations while you get some rest."

He strolled out the door as her world crumbled beneath her. How had they gone from him wanting her to be his wife to sending her away? Unable to support herself, her legs gave out, and she dropped to the floor. Beaten. Tears streamed down her face. Everything she fought for walked out the door, taking her heart with him.

The arrangements Paxton planned to make over the phone with Rocco turned out to be something he had to deal with in person. Rocco had flown in to help handle the situation with Gino if needed. Now, Gino wasn't a problem, but it didn't mean there weren't other things requiring Rocco's attention.

"What the fuck are you thinking?" Rocco sat his laptop aside and glared at Paxton.

"I don't have a choice." He didn't have the energy to deal with his boss, but since he was in Rocco's penthouse, there wasn't much choice.

"You and I both know that's bullshit." If there was one person who understood what it was like to walk away from a woman he cared about, it was Rocco.

"Come on, Rocco. You of all people should understand."

"Understand, you're walking away from your woman because you believe you can't protect her." Rocco shook his head. "No, I can't understand that. You love her man, you stick by her side and protect her."

"You've been here, you know this isn't easy."

"My situation was completely different." He ran his hands over his thighs. "I didn't have a choice, my papers for the military were signed. I was off to boot camp, and there's no way out of it. But when you have a love like you have, you don't let it slip by. You have to hold on and fight for it. You fight for her. What I had wasn't the same, obviously. Sending her away shouldn't be an option."

"Fuck, man! How else am I supposed to keep her safe?" Rage poured through every cell in his body. The idea of sending Bianca off with a new identity was killing him. He wanted her with him, but tonight proved he couldn't keep her safe. Even with Marco and Gino dead, it didn't mean the problems would end.

"I'm working it out now. Give me a little more time."

"The longer she's around me, the more danger she's in," Paxton screamed.

"You're the reason she's safe." Hawk leaned against the bar separating the living room from the kitchen. "You walk away from her now, and there's no telling what will happen. Think this through."

"I need some air." Before either of them could say anything, he strolled toward the rooftop stairs. Something was still off about the whole situation, maybe some fresh air would bring whatever nagged at him to the forefront of his mind. How had Gino got into the building? They had the place covered. There was no way he made it there before them nor any way he could have gotten past them. Leaving it a huge question in the investigation. How could he keep her safe if he couldn't even manage the small details?

Every moment of his time in prison, she occupied his thoughts. His goal had been to find a way out so they could have a life together. Now, he was out, and he was about to give her up. It didn't matter that it was to keep her safe; it still left the same outcome. *I'll find a way to end this and keep you safe. When I do, I'm coming back for you.*

Stretched out on the cool hardwood floor Bianca came back to reality when Paxton's voice ripped through the fog of her emotions. *The longer she's around me the more danger she's in.* What did he mean? Why was she in danger being close to him? She was the one bringing danger to him? Needing answers, she forced herself to get off the floor.

Thankful she still had her jeans around her ankles, she pulled them up and headed to the living room. The pain from her injuries protested with every movement, but she didn't let it stop her. Stepping out into the living room, she found Rocco reclined on the sofa and another man she had seen with Paxton when he came to rescue her but wasn't sure of his name, leaning against the bar.

"Ms. DeMeo, is everything okay? Can I get you something?" The other man moved away from the counter and came toward her.

"I'm…" She didn't know how to answer him. Part of her wanted to say fine but that was as far from the truth as she could get. "Where's Paxton?"

"He'll be back." Rocco answered. "Should I get Tanner? He can give you something for the pain."

"Everyone wants to drug me up." She shook her head.

"I've never liked how they messed with my mind." The other man came up next to her. "At least let me help you to the chair." When she nodded, he wrapped his arm around her waist, allowing her to use him for support instead of having to put weight on her injured leg.

"According to Tanner's report, you're going to have some nasty bruises. He suggested you ice them and rest. Yet, you're doing neither." Rocco watched as she made her way to the chair next to him before leaning back again. "What's on your mind?"

"Paxton." She leaned back against the chair. All the activity of the day caught up with her, leaving her exhausted. "I heard him before he left. He said I'm in danger because of him. What is he talking about?"

"He went in undercover. Do you not expect there'd be consequences to that?"

"Hawk." Rocco eyed the other man.

"But Marco…" She turned to face him. "You mean…" She couldn't even

132

get the words to come out. Her brain was firing on all cylinders, but it took her a moment to grasp what was being laid out before her. "No! Not after all this bullshit. Not after I almost lost him."

"Bianca." Rocco reached over and took her hand. "I told you before I was going to make things right so you two could be together. I got him out of prison and reunited the two of you. You need to continue to trust me. I'm working on this."

"Who took over for my brother?"

"Roberto."

Shit! This complicated things further. Being family meant he might want retaliation for what they had done to Gino. Every time she thought they caught a break, another block tumbled down on them. "That's Gino's cousin. I don't believe they were close but still blood."

"I've already contacted Roberto's second in command, and I'm expecting a call from Roberto within the hour. I'm going to make this go away."

"That's why you didn't involve the police. You're going to make it like Gino disappeared." She watched Rocco, trying to search for anything that might give her a clear answer.

"We didn't involve the police because this is family business. Just like the mafia world you've been exposed to, we take care of our family. We're normally on the right side of the law, but when we must, we'll cross that line if it means keeping one of ours alive and safe. You're part of that family, now."

"Paxton wants to send me away."

Rocco squeezed her hand. "Trust me."

She wanted to believe him, but the idea of everything working out was almost more than she could believe. Every twist and turn on this road had left her with more heartache. Everyone she cared about had been stripped away from her, leaving behind only Paxton. Now, the threats haunting her threatened to take him, too. If she lost him, it would break her.

Chapter Sixteen

More than an hour on the roof left Paxton with only one certainty and a whole list of unanswered questions. Giving up Bianca might be the best way to keep her safe, but he'd never been able to give up on anything he wanted. It didn't matter how much hard work it took to get it; he'd do it. The same with Bianca. He'd find a way to keep her and keep her safe. She meant the world to him and sending her off to who knows where with a new identity so she could live her life wasn't an option. At least it wasn't an option any longer. He'd make it clear to Rocco that whatever plans he'd put into action to get her to a secure location needed to be cancelled.

They'd have to find somewhere they could go together because returning to New York City didn't seem to be a reasonable option. Anyone after them wouldn't have to look hard to find them in the city. He couldn't keep her locked up in the condo forever. What that meant for him or his position with Phantom Security, he wasn't sure. Any case assigned to him would be at more risk because of the baggage he carried. Leaving his position seemed to be the only logical solution. Hopefully Rocco would still help him keep her safe. Rocco's words echoed through his thoughts: *She's become important to all of us.* Hopefully, that meant he could count on Rocco to make sure she was safe.

Jogging down the steps back to the penthouse, he hoped to catch Rocco before he turned in for the night. There were a few things they needed to discuss before he could try to fix what he just fucked up with Bianca.

Somehow, he'd make her see he had her best interest at heart when he tried to walk away from her. He just wasn't strong enough to give her up. She was his one weakness.

He pulled open the door and stepped into the penthouse. Rocco was still in the same chair he was when Paxton left, working on his laptop. As his eyes adjusted to the semi-dark living room, he spotted Bianca stretched out on the sofa, asleep. "What's she doing out here?"

"She was worried about you." Rocco didn't bother to look up from the screen as he answered. "Your girl's got fight. She's not willing to let you shove her aside and go off to deal with a problem she believes she helped create."

"She didn't do shit." His voice started to rise, but he tightened his control and strolled further into the room. "If you're working on getting her out of here you can quit, I've changed my mind."

Rocco glanced up at him, his eyebrow raised. "You changed your mind, and you think that's it? You can stroll back in, and she'll forgive you."

"I'll make her see." He glanced over at her, longing to go to her and pull her into his arms. "I'll have my resignation to you in—"

"Resignation?"

"Yeah, I'll have it to you in the morning. What choice do I have? If I'm not going to send her to one of the safe houses then I need to focus on keeping her safe. Plus, with the baggage I bring, I'm too much of a danger to be sent out on missions. I'm no use to you until I can deal with this or they put a bullet in my brain."

"You won't be any use to me then." Rocco closed the laptop and set it aside. "I won't accept your resignation. Part of the reason I came here is because I have some things we need to discuss. There are changes coming to Phantom Security, and after talking to Flash and Elise, we've decided you might be the one to take the lead on them. It's something I want to discuss with Bianca as well, so we'll have to wait until morning. However, I can tell you this, I spoke with Roberto, and he has no interest in either of you. According to him, things couldn't have worked out better if he had planned them himself. He's taken over the organization and is turning things back to the way Bianca's father ran them."

"The cartel and Pieces are still an issue." Paxton refused to allow himself to relax even a little, but the fact Roberto and his crew weren't a threat was a relief.

"Roberto has taken care of them. He's taking credit for killing Marco, and I've assured him we're not going to contradict that. If we do, the truce is off."

"Why would he want to take credit for Marco's murder?" He was missing something, but he couldn't figure out what it was.

"The official story is information of Marco betraying the cartel came to him, and he reacted. Ordering Marco's death was one step, and the other was paying the cartel. They've worked out an arrangement benefiting them both." Rocco glanced over at Bianca. "What matters to us is it keeps Bianca safe. For Roberto, it will keep the cartel from seeking retaliation. Everyone is happy."

"That's it, it's over?" Paxton ran a hand over his face, trying to scrub away the tension. "I've fucked up everything, and now, things work out."

"I doubt you've ruined anything. Does this look like she's given up on you?" Rocco turned back to Paxton but tipped his head toward Bianca. "I'm going to get some sleep. Talk to her. We'll finish the conversation over breakfast." Grabbing his laptop, Rocco rose from the chair and headed to one of the other bedrooms.

"If you give me a few minutes, I can gather our stuff from the master bedroom."

"Don't worry about it. Hawk, Grim, and Tanner have taken the other rooms. The rest of the team is at a hotel in town." Rocco paused next to one of the doors. "At one time, I believed I had what you have in front of you, and I let it go. Don't make the same mistake I did. She's willing to fight for you.

You must be willing to do the same in return."

Rocco's words weighed on him, except it wasn't the part some would have expected. He already knew he was willing to fight for her. Rather the part holding his attention was Rocco thought once he had a love like Paxton had for Bianca. What changed? When he learned of Rocco's past and the girl he left behind, it sounded like love. Now, Rocco doubted it. Something didn't make sense. "A problem for another day."

He strolled around the coffee table and crouched down next to the sofa. Watching Bianca sleep, he realized how close he'd been to losing her. Hours earlier, he'd stood in front of her watching her eyes as he broke her heart. Now, he'd give anything to take it back. The thought of losing her was enough to crush any ray of happiness in the future.

"Darling..." He brushed a clump of hair from her cheek, when she barely stirred, he rose and lifted her into his arms. Pressing her sleeping form against his chest, he strolled toward their bedroom. "I'm not letting you go."

"It's about time you realized that."

He glanced down at her and found her wide awake in his arms. "How long have you been awake?"

"Long enough."

Shaking his head, he kicked the bedroom door shut behind them and carried her over to the bed. "Spying on me, darling?"

"You and Rocco were talking, I didn't want to interrupt. Then..." She looped her arms around his neck.

"Then, what?" He laid her on the bed, but she kept her arms wrapped around his neck, forcing him to sit beside her and lean toward her.

"I was hoping Rocco could make you see reason since you wouldn't listen to me."

"I wanted to keep you safe, Bianca, that's the only reason. I love you with every ounce of me." He dragged his finger down the curve of her jaw. "I know

I hurt you, but that was never my intention. I guess I didn't think things through. I reacted to the idea of you being in danger and me not being able to protect you. This is my job. I protect people for a living, and yet I couldn't protect you. Darling, I failed you."

"Don't, baby." With her arms around his neck, she brought him down toward her. "None of this is your fault."

"You need to get some rest." He leaned back, pulling away from her so she had no choice but to unlock her arms from around his neck.

"Stay with me."

"There's nowhere else I'd rather be." Needing to touch her, he ran his hand down her arm. It wasn't enough, but it would have to do. He needed to slip out of his clothes that still had her blood on it. Then, he could cuddle her body against him. A few hours of sleep with his arms wrapped tight around her was all he needed to reenergize himself.

He rose from the bed and stripped out of his clothes, tossing them on the floor next to the chair holding their duffle bag. *Our bag.* He liked the sound of that. Soon there would be more in their life that was theirs.

"Could you help me?" She lifted the hem of the shirt she was wearing and unbuttoned her jeans. "I'd really like these off."

"I love stripping you out of your clothes." In just his boxers, he walked back over to her side of the bed and grabbed hold of the waistband of her jeans. "This is more fun when I know you're going to be screaming my name as I fuck you, but for now, this will have to do."

"I don't know. Maybe we could—"

"Not a chance, darling." He slid her jeans down her legs as he tried to ignore his throbbing cock.

"Seems like your body has other ideas." Her hand reached for his cock, but he stepped back and tossed her jeans near the chair.

"Doesn't matter what my dick wants. We both need sleep, and you're in no shape for sex." His gaze fell back to the purple bruises along her thigh and knee, guilt rushed through him. If he had stayed with her, she wouldn't be injured.

"Don't." She tugged the blanket up, blocking his view of her injuries. "It looks worse than it is."

"You shouldn't have them at all." He shook his head. "Shit, I should have put you in on the other side of the bed."

"Huh?"

"So I don't bump your arm in the night."

Glancing at the bandage Tanner wrapped around her bicep, she nodded. "Easy fix." She scooted over, lifting the blanket as she went.

He climbed into bed, pulled her close, and pressed his face against the top of her head. "You're mine."

"This feels good." She curled onto her side, draping her injured arm over his chest. "I'm going to miss this...miss you."

"You're not going to miss a thing." He pressed his lips to her head. "You're not going anywhere. You're staying with me. I don't know what the future holds, but we're going to face it together."

"What do you mean what the future holds?"

"Rocco spoke to Roberto. They're not an issue. Neither is the cartel, but the future is still questionable." Whatever was ahead of them they'd face together because up on the roof he realized letting her go wasn't an option. She was too important to him.

"You mean whatever Rocco wants to talk to us about? Do you think he's going to send you off on a job?" The concern in her voice had him squeezing her tighter to him.

"I don't know what he's planning, but I originally told him I was resigning, so I'm not even sure I work for Phantom Security."

"He refused it." She adjusted so she was facing him. "You're a valuable employee to him. He's not going to let you walk away because of the undercover mission. He agreed to it, making him as responsible for what happened as you are. Mayor Folger brought you and Phantom Security in on a suicide mission."

"I wouldn't change it, it brought me you. Now get some rest." He rubbed his hand down her back. "Next time you crawl into bed with me, I want you naked. I want to feel your naked body against me. Then, all I have to do is roll you over and have my way with you."

"Shirts are easily removed." Her voice was heavy with sleep.

"Next time. Sleep, darling. I'll be here when you wake up." He watched as she snuggled against him, allowing sleep to take hold and drag her under. He was exhausted, but the sandman wouldn't be enough to pull him under. Questions weighed on his mind. What was he going to do about Phantom Security? Missions would take him away from her, and he wasn't sure after everything they went through to get where they are he could stand a night apart.

Chapter Seventeen

Leaning against the kitchen counter, Paxton polished off his third cup of coffee, doing his best to push the exhaustion away. It wasn't working. The lack of a good night's sleep had finally caught up with him and now wreaked havoc on his body. He wasn't sure how much caffeine it would take to lift the fog hanging over his brain, but he had another ten minutes to figure it out before Rocco would be ready for their little chat.

"Want me to top you off?" Bianca neared him with the pot of coffee in one hand and her own coffee cup in the other. "You look like you could use it."

"Leave the pot. I'll finish it off and start another." He sat his mug on the counter and filled it to the rim.

"Did you get any sleep?"

"Don't worry about me, darling." He grabbed the tin of coffee and begun to measure it out. "I'm used to getting only a few hours of sleep."

"You're not appearing on top of your game." Rocco strolled toward them in a pair of jeans and a white dress shirt.

"Morning, Rocco, can I make you something for breakfast? Or would you like a Danish? Tanner picked them up from a local bakery this morning."

"Traditional morning after a mission Danish. We normally grab these or donuts on our rush back to New York." Rocco grinned. "I'll grab one of those."

Paxton lifted off his glasses and sat them on the counter before squeezing the bridge of his nose. "How can you be so cheerful? You've gotten less sleep than I have. I know because I heard you moving about, most likely getting coffee half the night."

"I had a few things that needed to be dealt with." Rocco grabbed a Danish from the box and went to the table. "Bring your coffee and join me."

"Don't you want to wait for the coffee?" Since Bianca had already added the water while he was measuring the coffee, he shoved the pot back underneath and hit the brew button.

"I'm fine." As Rocco waited for them to join him as he took a bite of his Danish. Once they both took a seat at the table, he sat his breakfast aside. "I'm sure you're wondering why I wanted to talk to you."

"Maybe more me than Paxton, but yeah." Bianca brought her coffee mug to her lips.

"Well, let me explain." Rocco leaned back in his chair. "New York has always been a city I've loved. The excitement and possibilities, but it's becoming challenging. Let's say it's become a battle of wills and while I'm not one to quit, I know the challenges of keeping Phantom Securities main headquarters there is taking more of my time than I'd like. Moving the main aspect of the organization seemed to be the best way to allow me to get back to the work I enjoy. Otherwise, I'm going to be chained to my desk more and more in the coming months."

"Is that why you're converting this old hospital?" Paxton asked.

Rocco nodded. "The one thing I've enjoyed most about New York was being on the top floor. The view was a must have, and this place will give me that. It will keep us close to Washington D.C. and give us a place that will limit the challenges I have to deal with. There are other reasons this is the perfect location, but those are the biggest."

"Does this mean you're transferring Paxton?" Bianca reached over and placed her hand on Paxton's thigh.

"The building has a couple months of renovations before the main areas are ready. Unlike in New York where we had other businesses in the building. This will be Phantom Security only. As you can see, I've taken the penthouse. Flash and Elise will be one floor below, which is nearly complete. There will be other condos for anyone who wants to make their residence here. Conference rooms on the second floor with offices for personnel on the third. Workout center and pool in the basement, and the first floor will be the reception area for Phantom Security to the right of the entrance and to the left, well that's still up for discussion. I know what I'd like to see there."

"What?" Paxton pressed when Rocco went silent.

"Bianca, you talked about opening your own practice." Rocco leaned forward, placing his hands on the table. "It would be an ideal space. The reception area can work with one person welcoming both clients. Besides the flooring and drywall, the cosmetic aspects have not been completed for that area, allowing you to choose what you'd like."

"Why? Why are you offering me this?" Bianca shifted uneasily in her seat, and Paxton took her hand into his.

"Our job is, shall we say, difficult at times. Occasionally we must do things we have trouble with later, whether that's guilt, nightmares, or whatever. I realize I need to do more to ensure my crew is capable of doing their job, and there's nothing they're hiding. If a mission gets fucked, I need to have the counseling available for them. I looked into your schooling and evaluations from your professors. Three of them were convinced you needed to consider working with those who suffered PTSD. I know you want to work with at risk youth, and there's no reason you can't."

"A couple years ago Rocco started encouraging Phantom Security employees to do some type of volunteer work in the community. Many of us started working with the youth in the area, hoping to give back and steer them onto a path that would lead them to be upstanding citizens. We put together a week-long summer camp for at-risk children. We break it down into different groups, allowing the week to focus on what appeals to each child. It gives them a chance to experience things they might not otherwise. It also gives us an opportunity to do something different." Paxton's hand slid over hers until he could interlace their fingers "I enjoy it."

"Which is why I'm promoting you." Rocco glanced toward Paxton. "I would like to have you as director of P.S.C."

"P.S.C?" Bianca glanced from Rocco to Paxton.

"Phantom Security Camp," Paxton explained.

"Really? That's the best you guys could do?" She shook her head. "You've needed a woman's touch for too long."

"Most of the kids refer to it as Phantom Camp, but you're right, it could have used a better name." Paxton glanced toward Rocco. "I appreciate the promotion. Is this what you meant when you said you wanted me to lead things?"

"No, but I'll get back to that." Rocco kept his attention on Bianca. "Besides working with my employees, the camp could use someone like you. You can use the space to work with the children of the area, or anyone you want. We can give each other what we need. I need someone with your skills, and I can give you the space you need to give back to the community and work with the children."

"Do I need to give you an answer now?" She ran her hand over the table. "I'd like to think about it for a bit and talk to Paxton about it."

"I understand. Let me know if you have any questions." Rocco's gaze shifted to Paxton. "As for leading things, I want someone to stay here and supervise the renovations. To work with the teams I've already got in place to get the condos furnished as they're finished. There's an old staff building further down on the property we'll use. We need more agents. Having them go through our own training school will be the best way to ensure they're ready for the job. The old staff building will host those attending the school, keeping this building secure. The course will be nine weeks of training and four additional weeks in the field for hands on. After successful completion, they'll be put into rotation. I need a man I can trust to handle that, and I want it to be you. If you accept, you'll be in charge of going through each application, selecting only the best, and interviewing them in person before accepting them into the program. We'll keep it small, six to ten per course. I have a couple teachers already lined up, but you can look over what I've put together and determine if you need more and if I'm missing anything. Hawk and Grim have agreed to work with anyone who shows promise as a sharpshooter."

"Sounds like you have it all figured out." Paxton eyed his boss, wondering why he had been selected for this position. Was it because of the undercover mission that had gone to shit? A punishment for breaking the rules and developing a relationship with Bianca while undercover?

"I'm sure you're wondering why I chose you. I can assure you Flash and I discussed you as a possibility for this before you went undercover. With your skills and training, you're a good fit. With your military and then police force training, you'll be able to ensure they're ready." Rocco shot a quick smile at Bianca. "With her by your side, you make a perfect fit."

"Me?"

"When Paxton interviews the applicants, I want you there. You can do your own interview if you'd like, or ask questions during the main one. Either way, I don't care. You'll be able to tell more about their mindset from their answers than Paxton or I could." Rocco's gaze went back to Paxton. "You've been through a lot, both of you, and this is in no way a punishment. I happen to think some time out of the field will be helpful for you, and it will also give you time together. The program will happen as often as we need new recruits, but in-between, those missions are still a possibility, so don't think we're taking you out of it. You're an important part of Phantom Security, and you're like family. Flash, Elise, and I have debated this every which way, and we believe you two are most useful right here. Within three months, I hope to have the organization completely moved here to Virginia. Four months at max." He pushed back his chair and headed for the coffee pot now that it was done. "Any questions?"

"I'm sure we'll have plenty but right now I'm overwhelmed." Bianca turned to face Paxton, the questions swimming in her gaze. Unfortunately, he didn't have any answers to give her, instead he squeezed her hand. They had a lot to talk about.

"I'm heading back to Washington D.C. for a meeting, I'll be back tomorrow. Meanwhile, think it over." Rocco poured himself a mug of coffee and carried it over to the refrigerator to add his vanilla creamer. "You can stay here in the master suite. If you accept the positions, two floors below will be your place. It should be finished in a couple weeks." He dug into the front pocket of his jeans and produced a ring of keys. "This will unlock every door here and in the staff building. Take a look around, and Bianca check out your space. Before I leave, I'll bring out the folder with the plans I've put together for the academy. I'll also leave information about the at-risk youth in the area and opportunities you'd have if you're interested."

"Thank you." Paxton looked down at his coffee mug, and no longer had any interest in it. The fog that had settled over his brain seemed to have lifted. "We'll have an answer for you when you return."

Leaving his coffee sitting on the table, he pushed his chair back and took hold of Bianca's hand. He didn't say a word as he pulled her to her feet and headed back to the bedroom. He didn't know what to say. Did she want to stay? He made his choice to work for Phantom Security years ago when Rocco approached him, but he didn't want her doing it out of guilt. If she wanted to take Rocco's offer, then fine, but not because Rocco had helped get him out of prison or because he helped save her. If she wanted to work with children, then she could do it anywhere. She didn't need to be forced to divide her time between Phantom Security and doing what she wanted. Before he could make any decisions, he needed to know what she wanted. If she wanted to walk away from the whole situation, leave Rocco and his company behind them, he'd do it without a second thought. They were like family, but after he almost lost her not once but twice, he wasn't about to allow it to happen a third time.

Chapter Eighteen

Discussions helped, but it wasn't until Bianca stood in her future office that she realized they were making the right choice. As much as she was nervous about the changes, it felt right. Moving to Virginia, leaving the big city behind, and settling down for a quieter life was the perfect opportunity for them to start over. All she wanted was a simpler life, and now, she had the chance. They could build a life there together. The question was would Paxton be happy there or did he long for the excitement he'd be missing?

"What do you think?" Paxton leaned against the doorframe watching her.

She wasn't sure what to say. She could picture herself at work there. After entering the door from the reception area, it was two large rooms. She could see the first one as her office where she'd meet with patients. Make it warm and relaxing to help put them at ease. The other room connected and would be perfect for her to store her files. A private area where nothing could be seen by patients. It was large enough she could even add a second desk and make it more of her style. A working office, where she could sit, catch up on her files and work.

"I see the wheels spinning." Paxton chuckled moving away from the doorframe. "You like it, don't you?"

"It's a bare canvas that I can put my own touch on. I can have the practice I've always wanted." She turned back to him. "Is this what you want? I mean, are you going to be happy here? Happy with your new position?"

"Darling." He closed the last few feet between them and wrapped his arms around her waist drawing her tight against his body. "I'm happy wherever you are. The location doesn't matter as long as you're there by my side."

"And the job?"

"It's a change, but I love a challenge, and I think it's something I'll enjoy. More important, it keeps me close to home, close to you." He dipped his head so their faces were almost touching. "I'm not done making up for all the time we lost. This will give us time to plan your dream wedding."

"Wedding…" Her mouth went dry as she remembered their conversation from days before. "I thought you were going to find a priest days ago."

"We don't need to elope. We can do this properly, just quick." His hand slid under the hem of her shirt. "As soon as we get your office complete we're going to make some memories right here."

"Really now?" She raised an eyebrow at him. "I'm not sure if I should be sleeping with a coworker."

"Coworker?" He let out a deep hearted laugh. "Darling, I'm your boss—at least until Rocco's here—I give the orders around here."

"Is that how this works?" She tucked her fingers between his belt and his jeans, tugging him closer. "Well, I guess we can play your little game for a bit, that is as long as you keep me pleased. Otherwise, there might be a revolt, and I'm not sure you'll like your new boss."

"Excuse me." Tanner stood in the doorway, waiting for them to acknowledge him.

"What is it?" Paxton asked.

"There's umm…" He shifted. "Bianca, Rocco's attorney is here to speak with you. He's coming up the drive now."

"Me? Why? If he's coming up the drive, how do you know he's here to meet with me?" As Paxton's arms tightened around her, she was sure he knew what was going on, but he remained silent, making her want to look back at him.

"Rocco should have been here to tell you." Tanner shifted uneasily.

"He was expected back an hour ago but got delayed, maybe he's here to meet with Rocco." She tried again, but from the way Tanner's gaze shifted nervously, it was obvious everyone in the room knew something except her.

"Show him up to the condo, and let him know we'll meet with him momentarily." Paxton ordered, before spinning her back to face him. "During my undercover operation, I came across some information. Your father left the house and restaurant to you. They're already in your name…"

"What?"

"The attorney your father left in charge of his estate is part of the mafia. With Marco running things, he never wanted you to know about your inheritance. The deeds were transferred, your signature was forged, and Marco took over the property. Appearing to you and everyone else as if he was left the properties. When they were actually yours."

"But Father's wife?" She couldn't wrap her mind around any of this.

"Was left their place in Italy, where she spends half her time. After Marco was found dead, Roberto told her he wouldn't be supplying her drugs, so she boarded a plane for Italy." He slipped his hand out from under the hem of her shirt. "He's here to fill you in on the logistics of things and will proceed however you wish. The restaurant is still operating—"

"The restaurant is a front for Father's main business. I want no part in it. I want it out of my name, immediately. I refused to be tied into something I never wanted anything to do with." She pulled back from him, but he took hold of her hand keeping her close.

"We'll handle it." He interlaced their fingers. "Hold on for another minute, I don't want you walking in there blind."

"There's more? Why didn't you tell me any of this?" She didn't like that he was keeping secrets from her, especially when it concerned her past.

"I found out when Rocco called to let me know he was running late, and it's not like I wasn't going to tell you. I planned on it after we finished our tour. Rocco wanted an answer when he returned, and I didn't know his attorney was going to show up, so I thought it could wait a bit." With her hand in his, he led the way out of her future office and toward the elevator. "I figured we had more time and for that, I apologize. Let's see what we can do about this."

She didn't care what it took; she wanted the restaurant and anything else tied to her father's enterprise out of her name. She wanted no connection to the mafia left for anyone to find. Soon as she became Paxton's wife, she'd be Mrs. Bianca Payne, and she didn't want a shred of evidence from her DeMeo life to seep through. A new beginning.

Two weeks was all it took for the attorney to deal with Bianca's inheritance. The restaurant had been sold to Roberto for a reasonable price, and the house was currently under contract. The only thing left to sell was her condo, and that would go on the market the following week. Everything was coming together.

Paxton and she decided it wasn't safe for her to travel to Chicago to deal with moving her condo or to go through her father's belongings. Instead, Rocco hired a team to pack and transport everything to Virginia. It was sitting in storage until their condo was ready. At that point, she could go through everything and decide what she wanted to keep. Anything she didn't want that had value could be sold or used in one of the other condos that would soon house other Phantom Security agents.

The one thing she knew she wanted out of the storage unit was her father's oversized, dark maple desk. It would be the focal point to her office.

Reminding her of the life she believed she had before he died, and the one she wanted again. She missed her father, but she realized if he had lived she would have always been stuck with his lifestyle following her. His death brought her freedom, while it had taken longer, it had given her Paxton.

With clipboard in hand, she leaned against the doorframe and tried to picture the space in her mind. The desk and sitting areas would be the main aspects. She was adding two large bookshelves on either side of the window to hold her collection of books, as well as decorative items. The painting was the last major step that needed to be done. Even as everything began to come together, she couldn't decide on the color for her office walls. If she wanted to have her office complete, she needed to make a decision fast, otherwise it wouldn't be ready in time.

"The guys located the desk." Paxton strolled into the office, his gaze scanning the room, before locating her near the corner. "You got lucky. It was close to the front. They'll bring it over tomorrow once your rug has arrived. This way, it won't have to be moved again."

"Great. It's heavy. As much as I would love to have it here, waiting is better." She tossed her clipboard down on the folding table one of the construction crew set up. "I'm still holding you to your word."

"What's that?"

"I want you to fuck me on the desk." Licking her lips, she strolled toward him. "Every time I'm in here, I want to remember you pushing me down on the desk and you having your way with me." Realizing something, she paused and met his gaze. "Unless it bothers you."

"Why would it?"

"I don't know, maybe because it was my father's desk?" It was just a piece of furniture, but it meant something to her and having it in her office seemed like the perfect way of keeping him close. Would it drive a wedge between her and Paxton? Would she have to forgo her fantasy of sex on her desk? It was unprofessional, but she wanted to do it there, where she could always see it. In those moments when she met with a client who left her feeling hopeless, it would remind her people could overcome anything in their lives if they wanted to. They had.

"It's wood and screws. It's not going to stop me from having you spread out on it, screaming my name as you orgasm. Everything around us has some history. When the furniture from my condo in New York arrives, look at the pieces. There are numerous antiques. It's no different."

"A man who appreciates antiques." She looped her arms around his neck. "Maybe you'll take me shopping to pick out a few pieces for my office."

"Darling, you know I'd do anything for you." He placed his hands on her butt, lifting her gently in the air, and she wrapped her legs around his waist. "Antique shopping is no hardship, but even if it was, I'd suffer through it for you without a single complaint."

"Why are you down here anyways?"

"I missed my girl." He gyrated his hips against hers, letting his hardened cock tease against her.

"And?" She tried to ignore what he was doing to her. "You told me you had a busy day. Something changed for you to come down here."

"I need to make a trip back to New York City." He gave her a moment, allowing his news to sink in. "I heard through a mutual friend, my old partner from when I was on the police force is leaving the squad. He needs a change, and Phantom Security could be the perfect fit. I need to talk to him in person, find out his reasons and what he wants for the future. We could use someone like him here."

"When are you leaving?"

"We not me. I want you to come with me." He ran his hand along her back. "You've found refuge here, but you don't have to hide out. Things are safe for you, now. Come to New York with me. We'll spend a couple days there. You and Elise can hit up some bridal shops and find your wedding dress. You're going to need one if you're going to go through with the wedding at the end of the month. On our way back, there's an antique store where I believe you'll find the perfect pieces for your office."

The idea of leaving the safety she had there frightened her, but staying behind while he was gone for a couple of days was like a rock in her stomach. There'd come a time when he had to go on a mission, and they'd be separated but this wasn't the time. She'd go, and she'd have a great time. With most of the Phantom Security team coming to their wedding in just over two weeks there was no time to waste on finding a wedding dress. "When are we leaving?"

"Tomorrow morning. I thought we'd drive. It will give us time, and we can stop whenever we want. If you'd rather fly, we can."

"No, let's drive." With her legs still wrapped around his waist, she pressed herself closer to him. "Earlier you implied you found me for other reasons. Is that still on the table, or do you need to get back to work?"

"For you, it's always on the table." Tightening his embrace, he strolled toward the elevator. "Until you have furniture though, it's not going to be in there."

"You could have pressed me against the wall and had your way with me."

"Could have, but I'd rather see your naked body spread out on the bed under me." He pressed the elevator button, and as the doors opened, he strolled in. "You're worth me taking time out of my work schedule for more than a quick fuck."

"Once things pick up with the training and I start seeing clients, we might need to pencil in afternoon sex." Wanting him naked, her fingers worked on the top button of his dress shirt. "I don't think I could go all day without these little moments with you."

"Little moments?" His eyebrow rose in question.

"You know what I mean." She gave him a bright smile as the elevator doors open, and he strolled through the penthouse to their room.

"Do I now?" In the bedroom, he sat her down on the king size bed and stepped back. "Maybe I should forget our little moment and head back to work."

"Not if you want sex from me again anytime soon." She teased. "You know I meant us taking a break from work to fit in time like this. Us time, not just a quick afternoon fuck. It's good for our relationship."

"It better work. I've already had business cards made up." He stripped out of his clothes.

"Business cards?" She pulled her shirt over her head and eyed him.

"My information on one side and yours on the other. It will make it easier when we meet with applicants for the training program. They'll have both of our information if they need to reach us. Your business cards for Phantom Security side arrived today, and the ones we've ordered without the company's logo will arrive tomorrow, I believe."

"I guess it's all coming together." She unbuttoned her jeans, quickly slipping out of them before scooting up to the middle of the bed.

"As soon as your polo shirts arrive with Phantom Security logo, you'll be an official part of the team."

"I thought I already was. Rocco gave me my badge and everything." She didn't think she'd need it until they explained the perimeter of the old hospital was closed off from the public. There was a tall chain-link fence with barbwire added once the hospital closed to keep people out. Rocco went further adding a security code gate and call box. She had to put in her code and scan her badge in order to drive through the gate.

Protection. At first, it seemed over the top, but as she learned more about the company, she realized it certainly wasn't over the top. They needed every precaution they could put into place.

"That's right he did. I guess you're not a prisoner here any longer." Teasing, he climbed onto the bed and hovered over her. "Darling, don't get lost in your thoughts."

"Why don't you help me forget about everything but you?" As she reached for him, his cell phone went off, stealing the moment. "Little moments...gone too quick."

"Whatever it is can wait."

She shook her head, knowing the truth. "Go ahead. Really, I understand. You can make it up to me tonight."

He grabbed his phone, quickly reading the text message that was on the screen. "I'm sorry."

"Can you tell me what's happening?" She tried not to get her hopes up. So far, he's been able to be open with her, but there would come a time he couldn't tell her something. She refused to allow that time to cause a rift in their relationship.

"Elise has been working with the limited security system and has finally been able to pinpoint where Gino got in. She sent the video to Tanner. We need to watch it and deal with it." He grabbed his clothes off the floor and began to redress. "We've gone over every square inch of the building and found nothing. Turns out, we were looking in the wrong place. He came through the staff house. There's a fucking tunnel running between the two buildings, allowing the staff to travel back and forth without the weather interfering. No one said a thing about it when Rocco purchased the place."

"I don't care how he got in, I just don't want it to happen again." She grabbed her shirt from the edge of the bed and slipped it over her head. "We got lucky no one got hurt, and the bomb he placed was a dud. We can't leave the possibility open for someone else to try. Next time we might not be so lucky."

"Don't worry, darling, I'll handle it." He placed his hand on her shoulder.

"Do me a favor and stay up here until I come back. Okay?"

"Why?"

"Call me overprotective if you must, but I want you safe. With the new security features installed to make the penthouse safe, I know no one is getting in here." Now dressed he sat down on the bed next to her and took her hand in his. "I don't believe anyone breached the grounds but now we know how he got into the building, I want to seal it up and the grounds searched. Promise me you'll work from here until I get back."

"Okay." She agreed, and he quickly rose, pressed a quick kiss to her lips, and headed for the door. "Don't forget you're going to have to make this up to me later."

As he headed off to deal with things, she was reminded once again why the protection was so important. Phantom Security was a high-end security company providing both private bodyguards to whoever needed it but also handling jobs for the government. Those were the jobs they needed to be concerned about. Not all of them were completely legal, often leading them into high risk territories. Their experience was the one reason Mayor Folger had come to them, the other being Folger and Paxton's family had been longtime friends.

How long until Paxton finds himself back in another situation like before? Instead of being placed in prison as an innocent man, he would be up on charges for something he did during a job. As possibilities rushed through her mind the fear barely rose within her. Whatever happened, they'd find a way to get through it. They'd overcome so much already; they could handle whatever life threw at them. His job was his life; it was what brought them together. She couldn't ask him to give it up. Not that she wanted to, she was part of the organization, now. It wasn't just an organization it was a family. *Our family.*

Chapter Nineteen

Being back in New York was different, especially with most of Paxton's condo already boxed up, but they spent little time in the space. He wasn't sure when he'd make it back to New York and wanted to take advantage of all his favorite places. It meant there was more time for him and Bianca. No one busy cooking or cleaning, giving him more time to show her the city he had called home for many years.

"Zayden's here." Bianca peaked into the bedroom.

"I'll be right there." Tossing the folder aside, he rose from the bed.

"What's that?"

"Zayden's final evaluation report." Brushing a hand along her side, he slipped past her in the doorway. "Are you heading out?"

"Elise is on her way down." She nodded. "Final wedding dress fitting, I can't believe it. A week from tomorrow is the day."

"The day you walk down the aisle and become Mrs. Payne." He stopped and took her hand, pulling her toward him. "You're never going to regret it." He barely wrapped his arms around her as the doorbell rang, stealing his moment with her.

"Kiss me, and go meet with Zayden. I'll be back soon." Without giving him a chance to do as she asked, she rose onto her toes and pressed her lips to his.

He knew he should keep the kiss simple and sweet except it was anything but. His tongue slipped between her lips, and he was met with the sweet taste of spearmint, making him want to explore further. Her hand pressed against his chest, not to stop him but to keep her balance. His tongue danced with hers, teasing along the inside of her mouth, before he pulled back. With one final kiss, he ended it. "There will be more waiting when you get back."

"I can't wait."

Without moving from the spot, he watched as Bianca strolled toward the front door. Her beautiful butt filled out her jeans as if they were a second skin, making him want to rush over and grab her again. Since they arrived in the city, their intimate time had been limited, making his desire rise to an all-time high. It was almost as bad as when he was in prison. Every cell in his body burned with need for her.

As the front door shut behind her, his opportunity disappeared. Silently promising himself he'd make up for it later, he headed toward the living room where Zayden waited. The evaluation report still running through his thoughts. *Loose cannon. A threat to the department's authority.* His previous evaluations were night and day different from the last one. *One of the best officers I have in my squad. Conducts excellent investigations regardless of complexity. Thinks outside the box.* He wasn't buying it; one assignment had changed him that much. He read the reports. He knew what they said without looking at them, but there was something more. Were they trying to force him out?

"Hey man, it's been too long." Zayden sat on the sofa, a smile painted on his face, hiding whatever was going on inside his mind.

"Too long." He continued into the living room before taking a seat on the recliner. "I heard you're leaving the force."

"Yeah, it's time." The hint of disappointment clear in his voice. "You did well for yourself. Maybe it's time I gave the private sector a chance."

"That's actually why I wanted to meet with you." He grabbed a package of information about Phantom Security and held it out to Zayden. "Phantom

Security is expanding. We're looking for people like you."

"You came into town for this?" Zayden nodded toward the door. "Risked your lady for a job offer? Yeah, I know all about what happened and who her family is."

"Was." Paxton corrected. "That life is behind her. She's not in any danger, and next weekend, she'll have a new last name, placing her past as far behind her as we can. There's still extended family involved in it, but she's not. I'd appreciate it if you didn't mention her past around her. It brings up bad memories."

"Like her brother putting you in prison." He shook his head. "Man, you should be glad it was under a false name. Do you have any idea who was in the same cell block as you? Tommy Cunningham. He'd have gutted you if he recognized you."

Tommy Cunningham had murdered seven people in Chicago before coming to New York. Paxton was only part of the team that had brought him down but for some reason Tommy had a real hard on for Paxton. No doubt if they'd have been reunited behind bars it would have opened up another can of trouble for him.

"I spent most of my time in the hole. I never saw him." He leaned back against the chair and took in the other man. "It would seem you've done your research on me."

"Like you haven't done the same." Zayden let out a deep laugh. "You already know I didn't resign out of choice."

"Why don't you tell me about it?"

Zayden's posture shifted, the muscles in his arms tightened until they strained against the thin material of his shirt. He reached up, racked his hand over his face, before dragging his fingers through his beard. "I don't know how much you know but here." He reached beside him and handed Paxton a small stack of papers. "Here's the report. If you still want to discuss

163

employment after you've read them, I'll gladly sit down with you."

"I don't want to read the official line. I want to know what happened."

"My report's in there." Zayden tipped his head toward the file as his gaze remained on Paxton. "Fuck no, man! I know what you mean, and it's not happening. You've been there. Once the job is done, we put it behind us. I'm not going to hash it out with you like you're a fucking shrink. I've been there and look where the results got me—thrown off the force. I'll tell you this, my actions saved that girl. If I had the chance to do it again, I'd do it. I regret the consequences, but I wouldn't change my actions."

Even as he said it, Paxton saw the guilt swimming in his eyes. The decisions Zayden made that day weighed on him. It was clear Paxton needed to know more before he could officially hire him. Elise would work her computer magic and find out anything she could, and he'd reach out to some of his old contacts to see what had been left out of the reports.

For the next hour, they went over what Phantom Security looked for in a recruit and what he could expect. As they spoke he realized something had changed in his friend. His attitude was darker, and he was more reserved. Still it wasn't enough to force him to change his mind. Zayden would be a good addition to the team.

"They knew." Zayden dragged his hand over his face. "They fucking knew."

"Knew what?" Paxton pressed.

"It was a multi-department take down, and they knew they were prostituting the women. A man named Lewis collected girls and auctioned them off. One of the guys we were watching, Black, purchased some in hopes of spreading his business to other avenues." Zayden dragged his hand through his hair. "I had just climbed into the surveillance van when he slit the other woman's throat. I couldn't stand by and do nothing. I didn't think about our cover or what could happen, I just reacted."

"Your reaction saved the second woman."

"How many others were in danger that we weren't able to save because of my actions?" He shook his head. "My actions resulted in a fellow officer being killed. I must live with that, but are you sure you want to bring me on? Shouldn't you talk it over with your boss or something?"

"Everything's squared away there. I've been at this for a while. I know what I'm doing, and I trust my instincts. You're going to be a valuable part of the team. But first—" As if on cue the door to the condo open, and Bianca breezed back in.

"Oh sorry, I…"

"It's fine. Come here, Bianca." He held his hand out to her as he turned back to Zayden. "Before I can offer you an official employment contract, Bianca, as the company's psychologist, needs to sign off on your mental health. Why don't you come down to Virginia on Thursday? You and Bianca can have your meeting then I'll give you a tour of the grounds. Afterwards I can answer any questions you might have, and we can deal with the contract."

"Won't that be a bit much with the wedding on Saturday?"

"It's a small affair." Bianca came to stand next to Paxton and took his outstretched hand. "I assure you it will be fine. I'll have time, and it will keep my mind occupied."

"You're attending the wedding anyway, so it's perfect timing." Paxton tugged on her hand, bringing her down so she was perched on the side of the chair, and he could wrap his arm around her waist. "Your conversation with Bianca will have doctor-patient confidentiality. She only has to sign off that you're mentally competent to do the job you're being hired to do."

"I figured. I didn't like the shrink shit before." Zayden glanced at Bianca. "I apologize, no offense meant."

"Don't worry, it takes a lot to insult me." She let out a light chuckle. "This won't be a regular thing, unless you need to talk. All new hires will go through this step, including those coming for the training course. However, if you need anything, my door's always open. Let me grab you a card so you have my contact information."

"All ready handled." Paxton's grip tightened as she started to rise. "Inside the folder, you'll find a card with our information on it. Mine on one side, hers on the other."

"Then I'll make my arrangements and see you in Virginia in a couple days." Zayden rose from the sofa and gave Bianca the first real smile Paxton witnessed since he arrived. "He's a good man and has been a good friend to me for years. It's nice to see him happy. To see you both happy. Congratulations."

"Thank you." Bianca stood. "I couldn't picture my life without him. He's my rock."

"Don't let her fool you, she's just saying this shit because I'm listening." Paxton joked rising from the chair.

"I'll let you two handle that on your own." Zayden chuckled and headed toward the door. "I'll see you Thursday. Oh, Bianca, your man tends to get a little annoying when he's stressed. Do me a favor, and don't kill him before I sign the employment contract."

Paxton shook his head. A least the smart-ass side of Zayden was still in tack, he wasn't sure he could handle the boring life again. "Thanks for coming; I'll see you in a few days."

He escorted his buddy out the door before turning around to face Bianca. "How'd everything go?"

"Wonderful." She grinned. "There was a small correction that needed to be taken care of, so my dress will be dropped off this afternoon. I'm all ready for tomorrow. Antique shopping." She nearly bounced with excitement.

"Since this is our last night in New York, why don't we get dressed up, have a nice dinner, and I don't know maybe dancing or a show?"

"I was thinking we might stay in." She reached into the bag she had been holding since she came into the condo and pulled out a sheer, red negligee with black lacy trim around the edges. "I'll change into something comfortable, we'll order in food, and well…"

"Food later…change now." He couldn't wait to see her in that, more like he couldn't wait to strip her out of it.

Chapter Twenty

Everything had turned out better than Bianca could have expected it. As Mrs. Bianca Payne, she could finally put her past behind her. She didn't have to worry about introducing herself to someone and them knowing she was related to the Nitti crime family. Payne was a common enough name; no one gave it a second thought. More than that, she was thrilled to be Paxton's wife. A few months ago, she wouldn't have expected things to happen this fast, but after he was arrested, she realized once she got him back she didn't want to spend a day away from him. She wanted to build a life with him. Little did she know it would become the life she always wanted.

Phantom Security's new home was coming together. In a few weeks, the Virginia operation would be up and running. The training course would be a couple additional weeks, as they finished the remodeling of the former staff building, converting it into dorms for those going through the training program. Besides interviewing each of the possible candidates, she finally started prepping for her own work. There was a list of things she wanted to get done before her first official appointment with one of the local children the following week. An even longer list for the upcoming week-long summer camp. She had so many ideas she wanted to put into action before then. She was going to make a difference. She'd bring something good to the world to replace all the horrible things her family had done.

"Your hutch has arrived." Paxton stood in the doorway, a line of paint on his forehead.

Seeing him there without a shirt and only a pair of faded blue jeans sinking low on his hips made her wonder why she was in the other room setting up the filing cabinets while he was painting her office. She should be out there, enjoying the show. It had taken her weeks to decide on the paint color for her walls, but she had finally done it. Vintage vessel, a mixture of blue and gray that seemed peaceful and beautiful. It wasn't a color that stood out, overpowering a person but would add soothing vibes to the space. She always loved the color gray, but it was too dreary for a place that would reveal too many troubling memories.

"So?"

"Huh?" She glanced up at him, meeting his gaze, and realized she missed something. "Sorry, baby, I was thinking."

"Thinking about how your office is coming together and my plans to celebrate? Or how many times I've already had you moaning and screaming my name in here?"

"Something like that." She grinned, tossing the file aside. "Or maybe I was thinking how damn sexy you look with paint on your forehead."

"I guess you'll have to make sure I'm clean later." The hunger in his eyes burned bright as she sauntered toward him. "Right now, I need you to tell us where you want it so the delivery men can put it where it goes. Otherwise Zayden and I will get roped into moving it a dozen times."

"You know, she's going to have us moving it at least five more times." Zayden chuckled as Bianca strolled toward them. "How many times did I help you rearrange your condo once your furniture arrived? Six? Seven?"

"It has to be perfect." She shook her head as the guys shared a laugh at her expense. "Didn't I loan him out when the furniture for your place arrived?"

"Really?" Zayden placed his arm at the top of the large filing cabinet and watched her.

"What? I did. I put off rearranging. I'll admit rearranging, again, so he could help you."

"Which you then came down to tell him how if he put this there and that there it would give him more space." Chuckling Paxton looped his arm around her. "I love you, darling, but you know I'm right."

"I also know men have no sense of taste. Who helped you get the oversized sofa into the condo? That's right, me." She glanced over at Zayden. "Otherwise your ass would be sitting on the floor."

"Helped? I think that's an overstatement. Directed…now, I'll give you that." Zayden let out another deep laugh. "Man, Paxton, you picked a feisty one."

They might be sharing a laugh at her expense, but it was still good to see Zayden laugh. It was so rare of an event that she didn't even care. Paxton and Zayden had been friends for years, but since Zayden joined them in Virginia, they invited her into their bond. The three of them were close, and since Zayden had taken over the lead trainer position with the academy, they would be working closely together. It was nice they had a bond that would allow them to come together as a team instead of separately. They'd get more done together.

She had only spoken with Zayden one time in her official role, but something she said seemed to have helped. There were changes in him, maybe it had been the change of environment or being around friends again. Whatever happened to cause the shift, it was nice to see this side of him. His smile and laughter seemed to lighten a room.

"Are you planning to leave them standing around with the hutch all afternoon?" Rocco hollered from where he stood in the main part of her office.

"We're coming." She stepped out of Paxton's embrace and looked at him.

"I want it on the wall backing this room. Is the paint dry? Otherwise you'll have to move it later."

"That's where I figured you wanted it, so I started painting there yesterday. It's completely dry. The wall behind your desk is nearly dry and the one between the windows is still wet." He started toward the door. "Let's get this moved in, then we're done for the night. Tomorrow, we can get the rest of your furniture moved in and finish setting up your space. Tonight, we're going to order in Chinese food, sit around the fire, drink beers, and bullshit. This is one of the last few nights with our small group; soon the rest of the team will begin moving in."

She followed him out, wondering how different it would be once the rest of the crew showed up. Flash and Elise had already moved onto their floor, one above the new condo Bianca and Paxton shared. Zayden was across the hall from them, making the floor full. The top three floors in the old hospital had been taken over by them and soon the other furnished condos would be as well. Grim and Hawk would be the next to arrive in two days. They would each take over one of the four condos on the ninth floor. Tanner had already made his home there as well.

The only one she knew from the New York office that wouldn't be joining them was Chelsea. Her so-called love of the city had made her want to stay and keep the office running as it always had. Bianca believed it had more to do with Brady taking over the New York office than anything else. Though it wasn't any of her business. If the two of them were going to have what she had with Paxton, they'd have to find it themselves. Pushing them together wouldn't give them the same strong bond.

Catching a glimpse of Tanner moving through the entryway to who knows where, her thoughts wondered to him. He had gone to medical school but quit before he could finish, choosing another path for his life, instead of following in his father's footsteps. The quiet agent was an important part of the team, but there was more to his past than met the eye. It might have been her schooling, but he intrigued her, making her want to dig into the puzzle.

"Why did Tanner turn down the job in New York?" She hadn't meant to voice her question aloud, but when Paxton turned toward her, she realized she had. "I mean I thought Flash and Elise might be the natural choice, but when Rocco asked Tanner, I expected him to jump on it."

"As Chief Operation Officer and partners with Rocco, Flash and Elise are too important to the day to day operations of the company to have them in the city when we're running the operation from here. They also understood the reasons behind the move, Elise even pushed for it."

Rocco came to stand next to her. "Tanner's training has saved lives, he understands he's more valuable in the field. He also enjoys the action. I knew when we asked him we'd be losing an important part of the team if he wanted the position, but he had earned it. Paxton's earned it, too, but the cost was too great to leave him back in New York. His ability to come up with a solution no matter the problem was something I needed here. He's quick to think of an alternative when we need one."

She tried not to let it show on her face, but she still believed there was something more. Something they weren't telling her. Instead of pushing it further, she let it drop and turned her attention to the hutch the movers were bringing in. Zayden took control of the situation, directing them toward the wall where she wanted it.

"His brother, Travis, will be joining us here in the coming months, once he is discharged from the military. I'm sure that's part of his decision to deny the promotion." Paxton brushed his hand along her arm and turned his attention to Rocco. "I was just telling her we're going to order Chinese food, sit around the fire, drink beers, and bullshit. You going to join us?"

"I've already got the beers chilling, and Elise sent Flash for s'more stuff. Get everyone's order, and I'll call it in. Flash can pick it up on his way back."

"Done." Paxton pulled a folded piece of paper from his pocket and held it out. "Thanks. While you handle that I can get cleaned up."

"I thought you were trying to make a fashion statement." Rocco joked. "Thirty minutes, and he should be back with food."

"I'll have Zayden start the fire." Paxton slipped his hand into hers. "Let's go get cleaned up."

"My hutch…" She shook her head. "Forget it. We both know I was going to have you move it again anyways."

Happiness filled her, and she leaned against him as they strolled from her office. Zayden would make sure the hutch was at least in the general location, and right then she didn't care. They had only a half an hour before the food was there, and she had plans of her own for that time, the least of them was cleaning the paint.

Lovers are not as important as family. Do not confuse his devotion with the bond of blood. You're nothing to him except an easy fuck. She hadn't thought about her brother in days, but as his words drifted through her mind, she snuggled closer into his embrace. *You were wrong, Marco. This had nothing to do with what you called family. This was true love. Something you've never known.*

"I love you, Paxton."

With his arm around her waist, they stepped into the elevator, and he pushed her back against the wall. "What's that about?"

"Nothing." She dipped her head, not wanting to explain. "I just wanted you to know."

"Darling…" Placing his finger under her chin, he brought her head up, forcing her to look at him. "You're my world, my everything. I love you, Bianca Payne. Now and always."

Marissa Dobson

Born and raised in the Pittsburgh, Pennsylvania area, Marissa Dobson now resides about an hour from Washington, D.C. She's a lady who likes to keep busy, and is always busy doing something. With two different college degrees, she believes you are never done learning.

Being the first daughter to an avid reader, this gave her the advantage of learning to read at a young age. Since learning to read she has always had her nose in a book. It wasn't until she was a teenager that she started writing down the stories she came up with.

Marissa is blessed with a wonderful supportive husband, Thomas. He's her other half and allows her to stay home and pursue her writing. He puts up with all her quirks and listens to her brainstorm in the middle of the night.

Her writing buddy Pup Cameron, a cocker spaniel, who is always around to listen to her bounce ideas off him. He might not be able to answer, but he's helpful in his own way.

She loves to hear from readers so send her an email at marissa@marissadobson.com or visit her online at http://www.marissadobson.com.

Also by Marissa Dobson

<u>Alaskan Tigers:</u>

Tiger Time

The Tiger's Heart

Tigress for Two

Night with a Tiger

Trusting a Tiger

Alaskan Tigers Box Set Vol. 1

Jinx's Mate

Two for Protection

Bearing Secrets

Tiger Tracks

Healing the Clan

Alaskan Tigers Box Set Vol. 2

Her Black Tiger

Tiger Trouble

Alpha Claimed

<u>Forever Creek Shifters:</u>

Forever Fight

Protecting Forever

<u>Crimson Hollow:</u>

Romancing the Fox

Loving the Bears

A Lion's Chance

Swift Move

Purrable Lion

Bearly Alive

Saved by a Lion

Furever Mated Box Set

<u>Stormkin:</u>

Storm Queen

<u>Reaper:</u>

A Touch of Death

<u>SEALed for You:</u>

Ace in the Hole

Explosive Passion

Operation Family

Marine for You:
Lucky Chance

Back from Hell

A Marines Second Chance

Tanner Cycles:
Until Sydney

Beyond Monogamy:
Theirs to Treasure

Cedar Grove Medical:
Hope's Toy Chest

Destiny's Wish

Leena's Dream

Fate:
Snowy Fate

Sarah's Fate

Mason's Fate

As Fate Would Have It

Half Moon Harbor Resort:
Learning to Live

Learning What Love Is

Her Cowboy's Heart

Half Moon Harbor Resort Vol. 1

United Homefront Ranch:
Destination Heaven

Phantom Security
Different Sides

Undercover Agent

Takeover Agent

Clearwater:
Winterbloom

Unexpected Forever

Losing to Win

Christmas Countdown

The Surrogate

Clearwater Romance Volume One

Small Town Doctor

Stand Alone:
SEALed Rescue

SEALed in Texas

Through Smoke

Through Fire

Starting Over

Secret Valentine

Restoring Love

www.ingramcontent.com/pod-product-compliance
Lightning Source LLC
Chambersburg PA
CBHW030256130626
46549CB00002B/558